THE DRUM

Michael Ward

First published in 2022 by Sharpe Books.

For Mum and Dad

Table of Contents

Chapter 1

Little Salisbury House, Strand, London
August, 1642

The Countess of Carlisle swept into the room, a three-masted galleon under full sail. It was ten o'clock in the morning but there she was, in an exquisite dress of crimson silk dressed with pearls, softly rustling as it kissed the floor on her voyage towards Elizabeth Seymour. The Countess always made an entrance, even for a mere acquaintance.

'Elizabeth! How good of you to come. I hope you are keeping well?'

She studied her ladyship as they exchanged pleasantries before moving to a window overlooking the rear garden and the Thames beyond. Lucy had been the darling of the royal court and the Queen's confidante. But now the King had fled London in the face of mounting opposition, both from Parliament and the people. Always politically astute, the Countess had switched her support to the King's opponents before his departure. How was she faring in her new world?

The Countess invited Elizabeth to sit by the window. 'Have you heard about William Harvey?'

Elizabeth gave a start. Harvey was a scientist whose brilliant theories on blood circulation in the body had prompted a correspondence between them two years ago. She now regarded him as a friend. What had happened?

'Oh, do not look alarmed. As far as I know, Mr. Harvey is in good health. But I'm afraid bad news awaits him. His lodgings in Whitehall have been ransacked. Much damage has been done.'

Elizabeth pictured Harvey's home, crammed with the results of twenty years' research. Her mouth went dry. 'Was anything taken?'

Lucy paused, her face mournful. Even she understood the import of her next words. 'I believe so. A gang was seen leaving with bags full of written notes, and others left strewn across the street.'

Elizabeth felt the air leave her body, and her head dropped. She pictured Harvey's reaction to the loss of a lifetime's work, the details of his dissections and findings painstakingly noted for future reference and publication. He would be shattered. 'William was not there?'

'No. I understand he is currently in Nottingham with the King.'

As Harvey's star had risen in the medical world, he had been appointed Physician in Ordinary to King Charles and was often required to attend him. At least he was safe. 'Am I right to assume his house was targeted because of his link to the King?'

'I fear so. Such loutish behaviour. Yet another inundation of the vulgar. Although Harvey does not help himself. I understand he previously described the King's opponents as fanatics, robbers and murderers!'

'Feelings are running high. Many fear what the future holds.'

Lucy scowled. 'What my future holds is a dull existence without the court. The sooner this argument with the King blows over, the better.'

There was a knock on the door and a manservant entered, carrying a silver salver. He bowed. 'A letter for you, my lady.' Lucy took the envelope, glanced at the writing and placed it on the table, as her servant retreated from the room.

'How apposite. It is from Mr. Pym, and I was about to mention his name.' John Pym. The leader of the Puritan cabal in Parliament opposed to the King and, it was said, Lucy's lover. Elizabeth had marveled at Lucy's ability to move her support from King to Pym in a heartbeat, yet still retain her influence.

'Despite Harvey's political persuasion,' Lucy continued, 'Mr. Pym does not approve of the destruction of his property and life's work. Such pillaging does the Puritan cause no good, especially when it will be reported extensively in the Mercurius Aulicus.' Elizabeth nodded her agreement. The rapid growth of radical pamphlets was now matched by Royalist newsletters that would jump on this news.

'His lodgings have been secured but others may attempt entry again, now it's known he's not at home. Mr. Harvey must be informed and any remaining papers secured and evaluated for their scientific value, awaiting his further instructions.

As you can imagine, John has limited contacts within the royal court. So he's asked me to find someone who could perform this task.'

Lucy's implicit proposal lay heavy in the silence that followed. Elizabeth had been waiting for a request. Why else would the Countess have summoned her? She was duty-bound to rescue her friend's remaining research, nevertheless she was dealing with Lucy Carlisle, arch-schemer. She evaluated the proposal under the increasingly impatient gaze of her host. Yes, she would do it, but conceal her misgivings from Lucy.

'You would like me to do this? But of course I will, and I thank you for entrusting me with this important task.'

In an instant, Lucy's glower slipped into a radiant smile and, reaching forward, she patted Elizabeth's arm. 'Thank you, my dear. I knew you wouldn't let me down. Mr. Pym will be pleased.'

Elizabeth breathed a sigh of relief. Granting the favour, on the face of it, was neither dangerous nor onerous, so she had escaped lightly on this occasion. Lucy kept looking at her, but the smile so quickly summoned was now fading into a puzzled frown, as she stared at Elizabeth's neck.

'My goodness,' Lucy whispered. 'Surely not?'

Elizabeth stiffened. What now?

'Forgive me, but may I take a closer look at the jewel adorning your neck?'

Involuntarily, Elizabeth's hand went up to her throat to clutch a large sapphire. She was infuriated to feel a blush coming to her cheeks. Silently she leaned closer to Lucy who gently lifted the necklace and held it in her palm, examining the stone closely.

'Yes, it is. How extraordinary,' Lucy commented, and her gaze shifted from the jewel to Elizabeth's face, all traces of radiance now absent.

'Elizabeth, where did you get this necklace from?'

Elizabeth's discomfort had been growing into alarm until she heard the peremptory tone of Lucy's question. Now resentment started to rise. 'It was a gift from my parents on the occasion of my birthday in April. Why do you ask?'

Lucy let go of the necklace and leaned back in her chair. 'Because this jewel was stolen from my collection, just weeks before then.' Another silence. The glower had returned.

'But how can you be sure? One sapphire can look very much like another, surely.'

'I can assure you that a well-trained eye like mine finds no difficulty in telling them apart. It comes from living with precious stones all my life, an experience, I assume, you have been denied.'

Elizabeth took a deep breath. 'I'm sure my parents will have purchased the necklace from a reputable dealer. If what you say is true, they would not have known it had been stolen.'

Lucy's face softened. 'No, of course not. But the item is mine, nevertheless.'

Another pause. Elizabeth looked at Lucy's implacable expression and realised that nothing less than a surrender of the necklace would satisfy her host. But that was not going to happen. She had to buy some time. 'My lady, I hope you will understand this has been a shock to me and I need to speak to my parents. Let me investigate the matter further and I will get back to you.'

'As you wish Elizabeth, but the jewel will now stay with me, its rightful owner, surely?'

This was difficult. She had no intention of returning the necklace just on Lucy's say-so. At this point, she was prepared to believe that Lucy was mistaking her jewel for the one that was stolen. But equally, she would not be surprised if the Countess had invented the story to take possession of Elizabeth's necklace, which had caught her eye. She had to avoid any suggestion of the latter, at all costs, because if she impugned Lucy's reputation, the Countess could, and would, ruin both her and her family. Tricky.

'My lady. I am grieved to hear you suffered an intrusion by these…these common robbers. Just like William Harvey's loss, it is evidence that our world is descending into chaos and lawlessness. I want to find who is responsible, for your sake and my parents. But, to do that, I must keep the necklace to assist my investigations. My first visit will be to the dealer who sold the necklace to my parents. I must show him the jewel to remind him of what I'm looking for.'

'Well, they certainly need stopping, that is true. They broke in and turned my bedroom upside down. Dreadful business. I felt violated even though, thank God, I was out of London at the time. Luckily they were disturbed by the servants, otherwise who knows what else would have been taken.'

'So, it was only jewellery?'

'Yes, and some gold plate. I have valuable paintings and porcelain, but they ignored those. Probably did not understand their worth. Well, Elizabeth, I know you will investigate this vigorously and urgently, so you can keep the necklace…for now,' and she emphasised these last words with another hard look, that Elizabeth realised would brook no further argument about ownership.

'There, that's settled then. Oh, and I almost forgot. There's something else.' Elizabeth's heart dropped. With Lucy, there was always 'something else'.

'I need to borrow that handsome young man of yours. Thomas Tallant. Only a small favour. Nothing too taxing.'

Chapter 2

Fish Hill Street

The large dray pawed the ground with its massive hooves. The horse whinnied and shook its head violently. Even from the other side of the road, Thomas Tallant sensed impending trouble.

Tom and his father Ralph were walking down Fish Hill Street, approaching the northern entrance of London Bridge. It was mid-morning and the streets were crowded with people going about their business and street-sellers pushing carts, shouting their wares.

'Not happy, is he?' Ralph murmured as the horse's handler struggled to keep control. 'Someone will be badly hurt, if they're not careful'.

As they got closer, the dray suddenly reared on its powerful back legs, knocking over the handler who dropped its reins. Sensing his freedom, the horse moved up the street. A scream rang out as the heavy post it was pulling slid forward, crushing a man's foot. Passers-by backed away and the dray, sensing their fear, reared again, eyes bulging, its mouth covered in white foam and spittle.

Tom moved forward but his father held him back. 'That horse doesn't know you. You won't get near it.'

The press of people coming down Fish Hill Street was pushing the crowd towards the enraged animal. Shouts of warning went unheard among the usual city cacophony - hammering from the nearby coopers' works, the bellow of cattle herded to their doom in Smithfield market, the cries of the ever present scavenging gulls, circling overhead.

No sooner had Tom and Ralph crossed the road than the dray lunged forward. Its thrashing front hooves caught a young boy full in the face and he dropped like a stone. A woman shrieked and the horse whinnied and snorted, its pent-up terror released as it charged. The post was moving again, with a harsh grating sound, yawing from side to side as it slid up the road. Two elderly men, trapped near a wall, were knocked over in the crush.

'By Jesu' Tom exclaimed, 'can they not stop it?'

Ralph shook his head. 'Only with a musket ball between its eyes, if it doesn't calm soon. Come, there's nothing we can do. We must move on.' They were walking back from the Royal Exchange with a large pepper order that Ralph was eager to fulfill. He picked up his pace and turned left into Thames Street, the shouts of alarm and frenzied whinnying receding behind them.

Tom shook his head. 'What do they expect, bringing animals from the country into London to work on the defences. Likely the first time it's been off the farm. It must be terrified by the noise.'

'And the smell,' Ralph sniffed the air slightly theatrically. 'The stench of piss, rot and burning coal, ah yes, always burning coal. Horses are sensitive animals, Tom.'

'It must have thought it was in Hades itself,' Tom replied shaking his head.

'But it's all for a good cause, isn't it?' Ralph added sardonically, as they continued down Thames Street towards the Tallant's warehouse on the north bank of the river.

It was now over six months since the King had deserted London, leaving his opponents in control. After years of disputes between the King and Parliament, the inevitable rupture had occurred, and now both sides were preparing for war. London was being transformed into a garrison, the old City walls repaired and gateways strengthened, posts and chains installed across busy roads, and redoubts bristling with cannon appearing at major entrances to the city.

'Do you not agree with Parliament's steps to defend the city, father?'

'To be honest, Tom, I'm not sure what to think. As you know, I have not been impressed by the King's attempts to run the country - his meddling in the church, his inability to curb the Queen's flaunting of her Catholic faith and, worst of all, his ruination of trade and business by debasing our coinage. But neither did I want His Majesty chased out of London by a Puritan junto, using the Apprentice Boys to enforce its wishes through street violence. Frankly, I resent that I must choose one side or the other, when I like neither.'

'So you will remain neutral?'

'Let us say 'uncommitted', and for as long as possible. My main concern is maintaining trade. If the King decides to blockade the Thames to starve London into submission, I will become a supporter of Parliament overnight. As we speak we have ships returning to England loaded with spices. They will not arrive until near the year's end. Hopefully, by then, this whole business will have blown over. But, if not, the Thames must be open, so we can land our cargo. If not, we will all be ruined.'

They arrived at the entrance to the Tallant warehouse and stepped off Thames Street down a ginnel running down to the river. A stiffening breeze was tugging at nearby boats at their moorings. Gulls were riding the wind, making swooping arcs over nearby London Bridge, their white forms contrasting against the dark grey clouds scudding westwards above him. A squall of rain was imminent.

Approaching the warehouse, they heard raised voices and entered to witness Tom's watchman Isaac in a blazing row with his bookkeeper Sam, standing toe to toe. Isaac's tall wiry frame was looming over the young man, his finger jabbing the clerk's chest to emphasise his message. 'You do whatever you want Samuel Barnes, but you won't persuade me it's right. And God help you when His Majesty returns. Then there'll be a reckoning.'

'Isaac! Sam!' Tom shouted. 'Whatever is the matter? This isn't like you!' The two men stepped away from each other, red faced, revealing the groom Andrew, who had been watching from the rear of the room, his mouth agape.

'They're fighting over sides, master, the same as everyone else.'

'What do you mean, Andrew?'

'Sides, you know. King or Parliament.'

Tom's mind returned to the time Andrew was beaten up on the streets by a gang of Apprentice Boys for refusing to answer the same question. That was two years ago, shortly after his return from India, yet the need to show allegiance continued. Nothing had been settled, and now the stakes were so much higher. He was weary with it all.

He certainly knew who Sam would support, as he had previously been in trouble working with London's thriving underground press, printing anti-Royalist pamphlets. But Isaac was a man of the old traditions. His belief in monarchy had survived the torture of his nephew Arthur in the Tower. He blamed his Majesty's followers, not the King, which, Tom had to admit, was probably right. Whether Charles would have stopped it if he had known was another matter. It was a miracle the two of them hadn't come to blows before, and it would only get worse as tension in the city increased. But he needed harmony in the warehouse.

'It's Sam, master,' Isaac complained. 'He's going to enroll in one of the Trained Bands and take up arms against the King.'

'Well, why shouldn't I,' Sam retorted. 'What business is it of yours who I support, Isaac? Why shouldn't we all have a greater say in how our lives are run. Parliament is elected by the people. It is our voice. The King must learn this.'

Sam's belief in the legitimacy of Parliament was common but far from well placed. As a sitting MP, Tom had been elected by only a handful of village elders in the Suffolk village of Dunwich, and it was much the same across the country.

'His Majesty has God on his side. He rules by Divine Right!' Isaac retorted. 'To act against him is treason. Can't you see the danger, Sam? When the dust has settled and the King returns to London, as he will, there'll be a reckoning. You mustn't be on the wrong side of the line when that occurs.'

Isaac's face was twisted with anguish. Tom saw he was fearful both for Sam's mortal soul and his neck. What did the future hold for them all?

Chapter 3

Bolton Hall, the Tallant family home

Tom turned his face to the sky, appreciating the warm August sun. His mother was cutting blooms from a nearby rose bush. Beatrix Tallant's garden was her passion and she was at her happiest among her plants and the summer buzz of bees. Her work done, Beatrix carried her garden trug to where Tom was sitting and carefully emptied a mound of pink and crimson blooms on to the table in front of them, and started sorting them. The scent was overpowering.

'What are you doing, Mother?'

'Enjoying myself,' Beatrix replied with a contented smile. 'This is my favourite job, picking the Apothecary's Rose for the house, to scent the rooms. I also use it in conserves but the season's ending now. This will be the final harvest.'

It was over thirty years since Lady Beatrix had arrived in London from her family home in Amsterdam, the bride of up-and-coming merchant Ralph Tallant. When they bought Bolton Hall, outside Clerkenwell, the garden was a tangle of horse grass and briar. After years of toil, it was now renowned for its beauty, home to plants from across the world, many brought to England on the Tallant's merchant ships.

'Look who I found loitering outside.' His father Ralph was strolling from the house, Elizabeth by his side. Beatrix rose from her chair to embrace their visitor.

Tom had met Elizabeth after her family moved into nearby Manor House and she was now a frequent visitor.

'Come and join us under the shade of the medlar tree, Elizabeth. It's such a beautiful morning.' Elizabeth took her place and Tom immediately sensed something was wrong. He looked at her enquiringly but she shook her head slightly and looked away.

'I have, today, heard of more trouble in Essex', his father commented.

Beatrix frowned. 'Oh no, Ralph. Not now. Don't spoil our peace.'

'But I would like to hear Sir Ralph's news, if I may.' Elizabeth broke in. 'I sense the world is changing around us, and we need to know how, and why.'

Sir Ralph nodded. 'A landowner, Sir John Lucas, was attacked in his home by locals swearing allegiance to Parliament. They broke in, running through every room including the ladies' chamber. Lucas ended up in Colchester jail! I heard this from a merchant, himself a supporter of Parliament, who was outraged. These vandals don't realise they are damaging John Pym's cause, and the Puritan junto doesn't know how to stop them. But why are we surprised when last Christmas these same louts were rioting in the streets, used by Pym to push the King out.'

'An inundation of the vulgar.' It was Elizabeth, speaking quietly, to herself. Beatrix looked at her, surprise on her face.

'Oh no, Lady Beatrix, that is merely what I heard in conversation, not my view.'

'So what do you think, Elizabeth?' Beatrix asked.

'It is such a fog of confusion, I only believe that, as usual, it is a battle for power, and the lives of men, women and children will be lost or ruined before the King and Parliament reach any agreement.'

'And in the meantime, I have a business to run,' Ralph grunted. 'Whichever side allows me to continue that, undisturbed, has my support.'

'What do you think, Tom?' his mother asked, her face taught with worry.

'I was shocked the King was forced to leave London to protect his family. Our monarch, not safe in his own capital city! Surely both sides would think again? Over half the MPs have now left the House in protest but, so far, to no avail. Will blood be spilt? What's to stop it? Pressure is building and I fear the unthinkable is now almost expected by an increasing number, which is very dangerous. If it requires a pitched battle to make both sides come to their senses, it will be a damnable failure.

Tom looked around the table, at the worried faces of his family. As he continued to speak, he realised the matter had been on his mind for much of the last few days and, now prompted, his thoughts and concerns were spilling out in a deluge.

'I am minded to offer my help to control the wilder elements, so we can calm matters and provide more time for Pym and the King to find a peaceful resolution. I have been told Philip Skippon, commander of the London Trained Bands, is an honest and experienced man. I might seek his advice.'

'A noble sentiment,' his father said, 'but I think you overestimate your potential influence as an individual, if I may say so.'

Tom bristled. 'Well at least I will be doing *something,* Father. I can't stand by as English Protestants prepare to kill each other. Catholic scare stories are raising tensions, but you and I know that Catholics are not involved. It's a lie. But, nevertheless, the poison spreads, inflaming the public, and people are choosing sides. You sit on the sidelines for the benefit of our business, but don't you see? There may not be a business left, if war tears the country apart.'

‘Do you really think it would come to that, Tom?’ Beatrix asked. ‘This country does not know how blessed it has been, to avoid the conflict that’s devastated my country and most of Europe.’

‘Of course it won’t,’ Ralph scoffed. ‘This current huff and bluster is to put pressure on Charles. We’ll get a few skirmishes, and then the King’s powers will be curtailed, which would not be a bad thing. But a war, a *real* war? Are you serious, Tom?’

‘But what happens if your father is wrong, Tom?’ Elizabeth interceded. ‘You will have to fight…and maybe kill.’

‘Yes I will, which I detest as much as you. That’s why I need to do all I can, now, to stop this happening. Father’s right, I am just one person, but I can offer no more than that, can I?’

Tom saw Elizabeth was still distracted and was anxious to find out why. During a pause in the conversation, he suggested they look at his mother’s latest creation, a fruit orchard, and making their excuses they left the table. Almost immediately she reached into the tie-on pocket on her dress for her pipe.

‘Are you all right, Elizabeth?’

‘No, not really. While you were away, I had a meeting with Lucy Carlisle.’

‘What’s she up to now?’

Elizabeth shared with Tom the news about William Harvey. ‘I have been to his lodgings and it is as I feared. His library is wrecked and most of his papers stolen. Years of work, irreplaceable notes on hundreds experiments and dissections – all gone.’

‘And the culprits have disappeared?’

‘Yes. But if they were thieves, looking for money, why take the papers? I suspect they knew of William’s connection to the King and wished to hurt him’.

'He knows?'

'Not yet. I have sent word to Nottingham. But he will be devastated. I searched the house and rescued a number of incomplete findings from his latest work. I have taken these home and paid to have his front door replaced, to avoid attracting other thieves. But I do not look forward to seeing him. He will be inconsolable.'

'Elizabeth. I am so sorry. I thought street violence would end once the King left London and the Apprentice Boys had won. But, having encouraged the mob, Pym now struggles to control it. They've had a taste of what they can achieve, and disorder is flaring up in pockets all over the city. Father's even heard rumours from Stepney of mutiny, and the navy joining the Parliamentary cause.'

'Tom, there's another thing. Lucy wants you to meet John Pym. He requires a service and Lucy has recommended you. Pym has helped us in the past, sending troops to repel the apprentices attacking your warehouse last year. So please see him and try to be helpful. I assure you, we do not want to fall out of Lucy Carlisle's favour.'

The two of them fell silent, reflecting on Elizabeth's news, but Tom sensed there was more to come. 'There's something else bothering you, Elizabeth, isn't there?'

'You're getting to know me too well,' Elizabeth half-smiled ruefully, and told Tom about Lucy's claim on her necklace.

'So what are you going to do?'

'I have been to the shop where Papa bought the necklace but it is boarded and looks deserted.'

Tom sighed. 'It's a common sight, particularly those shops selling valuable goods. Many of their customers left the city with the King and court. They're a tempting target for looters.'

‘I have written to the Goldsmith’s Guild, asking for their help. They say they will make enquiries into the whereabouts of the jeweller in question, but I am yet to hear back from them.’

‘I hope you do.’

‘I must. I will not be beholden to Lucy Carlisle for anything. Life would not be worth living.’

Chapter 4

Cheapside, London

Elizabeth entered Cheapside and enjoyed a familiar feeling.

The narrow route up Old Change from St. Paul's Churchyard was lined on either side with jettied houses, two or three storeys high, leaning into its centre. Even in summer, the street was cramped and gloomy like many in London.

As she stepped from Old Change, she knew what to expect, but it still exhilarated her. At four hundred yards long and fifty wide, Cheapside was the largest open space within the City's walls, and to Elizabeth it was like leaving a dark wood to enter a clearing in full sun. She reveled in the light and space now above and around her, even though, as on most days, Cheapside was heaving with buyers and sellers of everything imaginable.

She paused to catch her breath. She had entered the street at its south west corner, so her destination, Goldsmith's Row, should be immediately on her right. She had been told to look for an unusual sight, a group of guilded figures mounted above a goldsmith's shop, woodsmen riding monstrous beasts. She had no idea why, but at least they would be hard to miss.

Elizabeth set off, wending her way along a crowded pavement. She had not visited this part of Cheapside before but knew of the reputation of Goldsmith's Row, the finest collection of jewellery and gold shops in London, if not

Europe. She had expected sedate magnificence, but soon encountered a faded glory.

It was called Goldsmith's Row but she noticed some shops were milliners or silkmen. She then spotted a boarded up entrance, and there was another! And throughout her short journey, she was pestered by herbswomen and fruit traders, accosting her from their stalls in the middle of the street, pressing her to buy their wares. She was glad to reach her destination, stepping inside a narrow shop front with the sign of a bowl and spoon hanging above it.

She entered a room no more that eight foot wide, but forty foot deep, extending into the back of the building. At the front was a workshop, followed by a small partition creating a second space – an office, doubling as a consultation and viewing area for customers. A man was sitting at a workshop bench, examining a jewel closely. At her entrance, he stood up and approached her. 'Miss Seymour?'

'Mr. Cooke? Mr. Robert Cooke?' Elizabeth replied. The man nodded enthusiastically. 'Yes, that is I, Miss Seymour. Such a pleasure to make your acquaintance,' and he gave a small bow. 'You had no trouble finding us?'

'I have never been to Goldsmith's Row before, although of course I know of its reputation. I found it easily enough, but…'

'It was not quite what you were expecting?'

'Forgive me, Mr. Cooke, I do not…'

'Your reaction is perfectly understandable, my dear lady. It's true, we have seen better days despite the Guild's best efforts.'

'That terrible press of small traders outside. I could not see some of the goldsmith displays.'

'Every week we push them back into the middle of the street and every week they encroach again.'

'And why are some of your shops not occupied?'

'It is a long story but, put at its simplest, it is another example of the malaise besetting this country. The Guild has done everything in its powers to retain the exclusivity of Goldsmith's Row and control standards among goldsmiths and lapidaries in London. We've even petitioned the Privy Council and Parliament. But we have received little support, just as in our attempts to control the market traders, so now anyone can call themselves a goldsmith and set up anywhere in the city. We have lost control of the situation, like so many others these days.'

It seemed to Elizabeth that the current crisis was reaching into every corner of London life. No one was immune from the fear and disruption it brought. 'You mean the dispute between King and Parliament?'

'Absolutely, and neither of those parties have helped the Guild either, I can tell you. Both have bled us dry with tithes, taxes and demands for contributions to fund their fight. As a result the Guild has been forced to borrow money and our finances are in a parlous state.'

'Well, it is good of you to see me Mr. Cooke, when you have so much else to occupy you.'

'Not at all, Miss Seymour. A request on behalf of the Countess of Carlisle is not to be ignored.'

Elizabeth smiled. Lucy may have wanted the matter kept private but fortunately she did not stipulate her name was not to be used, a name that would open any goldsmith's door in London.

Elizabeth looked around the small workshop. 'I see you do not use your window for display?'

'Lapidaries cannot work without the best possible light so they sit at the bench below the window. It makes it clear to passers-by what we do, and intrigues some, attracting their interest, which is always good for trade. Here, come and take a look,' and he walked towards one of the two men sitting at the workbench. 'Matthew here is examining a stone for imperfections, a frequent job for him'.

Elizabeth admired a striking amethyst in the lapidary's hand. She thought back to her visit to Bolton Hall. The jewel was almost the size of Beatrix's medlar fruit and, caught in the afternoon sunlight, pulsed with an intense purple hue.

'He is looking for any imperfections before he starts to cut the stone.'

'But why cut it? To me it is perfect!' Elizabeth exclaimed.

Robert Cooke lent back from examining the gem and smiled. 'I see you share my love of natural stones, Miss Seymour. However, if I am to make a living, my lapidary must fashion these natural marvels into shapes that will fit brooches, necklaces and earrings. It is highly skilled work. This amethyst comes from Goa in India, but soon it will adorn the wife of an earl, here in London.'

'And hopefully not end up in a thief's pocket some weeks later,' Elizabeth muttered.

'Ah yes. The reason for your visit. I am grieved, but not surprised, to hear of Lady Carlisle's misfortune. This is the third such theft to come to my attention in the last two months. One was from another private collection and the other a jewel merchant.'

'So, very different targets?'

'Indeed. A large number of finished pieces, some of considerable value, were taken from the private collection. However, the merchant's haul was mainly uncut stones, including a large number of garnets.'

Elizabeth hesitated before asking her next question. 'Does that suggest the thief may himself be a jeweller, Mr. Cooke?'

Cooke sighed. 'Yes, I'm afraid it is a possibility, Miss Seymour. A lapidary's skills would be needed to turn the garnets into jewels, but it would be worth the effort.

Garnets are particularly popular. As well as their beauty, some believe they have medicinal qualities, from curing watery eyes to stopping bad dreams! I do not subscribe to such theories, myself.'

'But you don't dismiss them?'

'Not to my customers, no. It may give them some comfort, and the stones certainly *do* enhance one's appearance, so they undoubtedly benefit from wearing them,' he chuckled softly.

Elizabeth was warming to Mr. Cooke. She had half expected a defensive spiky response to her questions but this quietly spoken and mild mannered jeweller was also open and confident enough to make fun of himself and his profession.

'You said you weren't surprised to hear about the break-in. So they are common?'

'Not on this scale, until recently. Usually jewellery is most vulnerable when worn outdoors, not locked away in a house or merchant's strongbox. Single pieces are prey to light-fingered thieves in a busy street or society ball.' Elizabeth raised her eyebrows. 'Oh yes, Miss Seymour. Always keep an eye on the servants if you attend a reception wearing your best. But these recent break-ins are different. They select their victims carefully but, once chosen, act decisively.'

'You must inform me as soon you hear of any others,' Elizabeth interrupted.

'You can be sure I will, and the gang may provide you with a wealth of evidence. They do not tread lightly, smashing windows and doors and confronting anyone in their way. A servant at the private house is still recovering from a brutal assault.'

'Well, that doesn't sound like the work of a lapidary.'

'Don't be too sure. Our profession has always attracted an undesirable element because of the materials we deal in. However, because we have been unable to regulate as we wish, there has been an increase in unscrupulous, dangerous men who ply our profession. Still we must continue as best as we can and if I can help I will. Have you brought the necklace in question with you? May I inspect it?'

Elizabeth retrieved the gems from a small bag at her waist. Cooke held the sapphire at the centre of the necklace up to the light and then examined it closely under a magnifying glass.

'Hmm, well it looks very fine, considering it is flawed.'

'Flawed?' Elizabeth exclaimed.

'Yes, I'm afraid so. If you look closely around the edge of the stone, can you see a silver edge? Here, use the glass. It's only just visible in several places. This stone has been 'foiled' – a thin layer of metal placed under the stone to intensify its colour and hide the imperfections present. It's been skillfully done but nevertheless it must be classified as flawed, I'm sorry to say.'

'Because it has been interfered with? But isn't that what your man is doing now?'

'Lapidaries cut stones to bring forth their internal beauty, not hide their flaws. It's a different matter, entirely. No, I'm afraid your jewel is flawed, Miss Seymour.' The jeweller paused and gave Elizabeth a wry smile.

'But it could have been worse. I was half expecting a forgery. Counterfeit sapphires are plentiful on today's market.'

Chapter 5

The House of Commons

Thomas strode up the steps of St. Stephen's Chapel in the shadow of Westminster Hall and nodded a greeting to the Serjeant at Arms. Reached from the Old Palace Yard, the chapel had served as the House of Commons for over a hundred years, since the days of Henry VIII's son, Edward VI. It was ideally positioned in the heart of Westminster, near to the House of Lords, and on busy days you could not find a seat.

However, today the Commons was deserted. Two women were cleaning the floor, their voices echoing in the chapel. He recalled the raucous debates he had witnessed in this room. In the current turmoil, it was strange to find it empty, almost desolate. Parliament was in session, but with no debate listed for today and many committees moved to other buildings, he had the Commons almost to himself.

A familiar figure was sitting on one of the front benches. Tom had met Sir Bartholomew Hopkins when he had become a member of parliament over two years ago. They had become close friends, a bond that had remained despite Barty's strong support for the King. A surge in recent trading had kept Tom from Parliament for some time, and he requested a meeting with Barty to catch up on events.

They embraced, Barty's eyes sparkling with good humour as ever, though his brow was furrowed. 'It's helpful the Chamber is deserted, Tom. It's easier for me to talk openly. Factions in the House are growing, rapidly. The Puritan junto leading the opposition to the King has been emboldened by his decision to quit London. What a calamity that was - to hand over the Royal Mint and the country's biggest arms store in the Tower to his enemies.

'But now Pym and his supporters have overplayed their hand, creating 'nineteen propositions' the King must approve to avoid civil war! Civil war? Who wants that? If Charles agreed he would lose any meaningful power. No, the moderates are deserting Parliament in their droves. Attendance has dropped by over a half.'

On the face of it, Barty's news was alarming. But the Commons was a hothouse of gossip and rumour. It was easy to lose a sense of perspective. 'I'm not sure it's as bad as you say. Challenging the King's right to rule does not sit easily with many Englishmen.'

'But as the hard core push further, they fear stepping back,' Barty replied, 'because they know what awaits them if they fail. Certain death, and agony before. When both sides shout 'treason', who has most reason to quake?'

'I agree tensions have been raised. But once people understand the road they travel is putting Protestant against Protestant, in armed conflict, they will come to their senses. There's no appetite for it, I'm convinced.'

'I hope you're right Thomas, but many seem crystal clear about their intentions. As we speak, hundreds are sailing back home from New England to join the Parliamentary cause.

He thought about his brother Peter, currently working in America to establish Puritan communities, and shuddered. Were his words of reassurance for Barty, or himself? They were beginning to sound a little empty given the mounting evidence confronting him. He would continue to maintain a brave face, but for how much longer?

'Well, thank you for keeping me informed Barty. We will need to keep a close eye on matters. Now, I have another meeting to attend in the House.' Tom had chosen St.

Stephen's because he was also meeting John Pym. He would not tell his friend that, and he knew that Barty's immaculate manners would never allow him to ask. It was a perfectly safe juxtaposition.

'Just so, and I have a dinner engagement on the Strand, so I will bid you farewell,' and embracing Tom warmly, he walked towards the front door.

Tom waited until Barty had left before heading for a small group of offices in one corner of the chamber. He stopped at the final door, knocked and entered. Two men stood in conversation in the middle of the room. One with his back to Tom turned, and the serious features of John Pym broke into a rare smile.

The leader of the Puritan group in Parliament stepped forward with his hand extended. 'Ah Mr. Tallant, is it not? Thomas Tallant, Sir Ralph's son?' The sight of Pym's face, his neatly combed collar-length hair and watchful eyes, took Tom back to that fateful occasion in the Commons when the Puritan leader escaped capture by the King. As on that day, he was dressed in black, with his shirt's large white lapels lying on top of his coat, covering his shoulders. He always dressed this way, like a uniform. Pym dismissed the other man from the room and guided Tom to a pair of chairs.

'I'm surprised you recognised me, Mr. Pym. There are so many members of Parliament.'

'Oh, I am hardly likely to forget, given the timely service you rendered me, delivering Lady Carlisle's warning. Otherwise I would not have known that the King was approaching the Commons seeking my arrest.'

Tom thought back to that day and smiled. He was not aware of its importance at the time, but that message was now earning him an audience with the man at the centre of the nation's affairs. 'Nevertheless, I'm intrigued to know why you have taken time from your many pressing matters to speak to me.'

Pym paused and frowned. He leaned forward in his chair, elbows resting on his knees, fingers of both hands intertwined. 'Yes Tallant. You are right. The affairs of state are pressing and at a critical stage, and I need your assistance with a particularly worrying matter. As you know, the King has deserted London and, as we speak, is in Nottingham attempting to raise a traitorous army.'

'The King – a traitor?' Tom's questioning expression made Pym flush. His voice became more strident.

'How else can we describe an army recruited to overturn the sovereignty of Parliament, elected and so authorised by his own people?'

Tom recalled his father's scepticism about war. 'Are you sure he *is* taking such steps? Perhaps it is a bluff to get you to step back.'

Pym calmed his voice. 'People are understandably confused. Taking up arms against their King is unnatural to many. But, let me assure you, as we speak, *he* is taking up arms against *them*! And this is why I need your help. Come and look at this.' Pym rose and walked to his desk, covered by a map of London. 'The King's flight from London was a decision made in haste, which he is now repenting at his leisure. If he had no thoughts of creating an army then, he certainly has now.'

'How do you know, with such certainty?'

'Gunpowder, Mr. Tallant.'

'Gunpowder?

'Much of the manufacture of arms and gunpowder is centred in and around London,' he continued, pointing at the map. 'Here at the Tower, and over here at the Minories, among other locations. You see? And crucially, all are currently in Parliament's possession. By fleeing London, at a stroke, the King cut himself off from the means of equipping his army. This he now realises…so he's attempting to steal said means from under our noses! Our intelligencers have discovered a group of Royalists, preparing to smuggle a large consignment of stolen gunpowder out of London. The gates along the city wall are closely guarded and it would be impossible to transport such a sizeable load on that route. Taking it out piecemeal would be too risky. Too many opportunities for discovery.'

'So you think they will ship it out?'

'Precisely, probably under the cover of night. I am told you have an unrivalled knowledge of the docks and wharves along the north side of the river. If we can avail ourselves of this, it would be most helpful.'

An unrivalled knowledge of the river? He recognised a typically overstated Lucy Carlisle flourish in his description, to make her contact with Tom more valuable to Pym. Every conversation for her was a transaction. What a dreadful way to live.

'I doubt a King with peaceful intentions would have need of so much gunpowder,' Pym continued. 'No, we must thwart this plot to avoid a bloody conflagration.'

'But how did they acquire it?'

'I suspect they paid handsomely, bribing workers at the powder mills to turn a blind eye. It will have taken months to accumulate enough for this shipment. It will be a goodly amount, and it must be stopped. Will you help?'

Pym returned to his seat and said nothing. Tom remained at the map, studying the long row of quays and wharves stretching from London Bridge eastwards towards the mouth of the Thames. Avoid a bloody conflagration… he recalled what he said to his family about doing everything possible to stop war. This would make a difference.

'Well, I'll need help to cover such a large area. Where shall I start?'

'Do you know Philip Skippon?'

'I have heard of him, yes.'

'He's a good and godly man. I will instruct him to provide assistance. Keep him informed of any progress you make, and only him. Do not talk to others. We need to keep this investigation as secret as possible. Understand? Good. Now, if you'll excuse me, Tallant…'

Pym bent over his papers. Tom's agreement secured, the meeting was over.

Chapter 6

Whitehall, London

Elizabeth stared at the rain falling steadily outside her carriage, then glanced at the leather satchel on the seat next to her. It contained the notes she had rescued from William Harvey's ransacked house. She was travelling to Whitehall to return his possessions now he had returned to London. Thankfully they would remain dry in her bag.

Twenty minutes later she was sitting by a warm fire in Harvey's lodgings, appreciating a goblet of warmed wine.

'Did I retrieve anything of value, William?'

Harvey gave a distracted grunt. He was shuffling through documents feverishly, shaking his head, his brow furrowed. Eventually he tossed the papers on the table in front of him and leaned back in his chair. 'There are some useful notes here from my recent experiments on circulation…'

'But?' Elizabeth ventured.

'I will be forever grateful for what you have done, Elizabeth, but seeing these reminds me how much has been taken. This…this is a drop in the ocean, but welcome nonetheless.'

'So, you've lost everything?'

Harvey nodded his head, his eyes filling with tears. 'My life's work. I wish it had been stolen by a jealous rival. At least it would be preserved in the wider body of knowledge. Instead, I've no doubt it has gone up in smoke or been dumped in the river.'

Elizabeth looked around the room, at the new doorframe and lock. 'My neighbour discovered a number of my sketches - of the heart and its function - scattered by his front door,' Harvey continued. 'These oafs had no understanding of, or interest in, the value of what they had taken, just like those physicians who derided my work when it was first published. Called me crack-brained! I am destined to be either reviled or trampled underfoot by the ignorant. Thank God I still have the King's respect, the honour to serve him.'

'Do you think you were singled out because you're in the King's service?'

'Why else? That's enough for some of these brutes. This is why we cannot give way to them. The King has no choice but to raise his standard and call those of who have retained their sense of loyalty and duty to rally by his side. This madness will not go away on its own. It must be fought, and stamped out!'

This was a different William Harvey for Elizabeth, and she was taken aback.

'But what of the cost in lives and human suffering? I believe there is a new movement starting, a Peace party, who continue to believe this dispute can be settled by reason…'

'My dear Elizabeth, reason deserted this Parliament many months ago. Was this an expression of reason?' and he swept his hand across the empty shelves in the room.

Elizabeth lowered her head. 'I feel for your loss, William, I really do. Nevertheless I believe the Peace party offers hope to us all, to stop the ghastly spectre of Englishmen killing each other - brothers, fathers, friends. We need to find out more about it!'

It was Harvey's turn to look surprised as he regarded his young friend, her eyes shining, her voice determined. He spoke again, more softly. 'Well, as we know Elizabeth, it is always good to learn, but I fear your time will be wasted if you attempt to apply reason and logic to the actions of these…animals. Your skills would better devoted to helping those who will be injured in the inevitable conflict to come. I intended to mention this while you were here.'

'What do you mean, William?'

'Thanks to the King and his father before him, for decades we have been spared the ravages of fighting which have destroyed much of Europe. Regrettably, the art of war has advanced greatly, in particular the use of gunpowder, muskets and cannon. If we go to war, the generals on both sides will deploy these new weapons to gain advantage. I fear it will cause much injury and suffering.'

'Why are you telling me this? It is exactly what I am opposed to.'

Harvey reached over and gently laid his hand on Elizabeth's. 'I am merely suggesting you spare a measure of the time you will waste failing to stop the inevitable, and devote it to a thing of real value - learning how to treat the new injuries these weapons will produce. There are several books I can lend you, written by physicians who tended the wounded in the German war. They are most instructive. Burns, for example are now more common, and I know of your expertise in preparing effective lotions.'

'You're saying I may gain something of value from any war which afflicts us? That I should see it as an… an opportunity?'

'T'was ever thus,' Harvey nodded with a sad smile. 'And as scientists, we should never miss an opportunity to improve our knowledge, for the benefit of mankind.'

Chapter 7

Finsbury Fields, North London

The sound of canvas flapping in the wind made Tom look up. The sky was pure blue and a fresh breeze was picking up, catching the sails of the two windmills to his left. Soon the sails would be unlocked to grind corn. He gazed across the large field at hundreds of men marching up and down, following shouts of command from their officers. Order would occasionally collapse into jumble of bodies. Laughter drifted across the field as the men re-formed in line, and the drilling started again.

Tom had arranged to meet Philip Skippon by the Finsbury windmills and noticed a mounted figure approaching, cantering across the grass, hooves drumming on the ground. Commander Skippon pulled up beside him and touched his hat. 'Mr. Tallant?'

Tom nodded and leant over in his saddle to shake his hand. He looked at his face, shoulder length hair parted to one side framing a generous moustache and a small patch of beard below his bottom lip, in the style of the King. Tom guessed he was about forty years old, a soldier half his life, fighting the Spanish in the Palatine and the United Provinces. He would know how to turn the Trained Bands into soldiers.

Skippon examined the hive of activity across Finsbury Fields with a practiced eye. Men were everywhere, marching, conducting pike drills or discharging muskets in the firing butts. He turned in his saddle to face Tom. 'I understand you have offered your assistance to John Pym. I am happy to do all I can to assist you in your task. I think you will find the two men I have seconded from the Trained Bands will prove useful. I've told them to report to your warehouse on the Thames. Henry Appleyard is a good soldier – dedicated and diligent. Don't be afraid to work him hard!'

Tom nodded his thanks. 'Just as you are working your men hard. Your forces have grown rapidly, Mr Skippon,' Tom said. 'The Trained Bands are becoming formidable.'

The Commander gave Tom a wry smile. 'We will soon number eight thousand so we are numerous, but far from formidable; not yet, at least. We have no shortage of raw recruits but now we must instill order and discipline. The safety of London may well depend on these men in the months to come.'

'Yes, I have heard reports of unruly behaviour in Essex and other places.' Tom was not sure how Skippon would react to this criticism. He expected protestations of innocence, perhaps outrage, but was surprised by his answer.

Yes, I'm afraid this is true. Many of Parliament's supporters have become accustomed to the excitement on the streets. Creating chaos has been their main weapon so far, but that will be of no help on the battlefield. I spent many years fighting in Germany and I tell you war brings more than enough of its own chaos. These men need unity of purpose and deed, shaped into a single body, a fighting machine, and we don't have much time.'

'And you think it will come to this…to war?'

'I pray not, with all my heart,' and here he reached into his saddlebag to retrieve a well-thumbed copy of a Breeches Bible, lifting it in his hand. 'I pray for peace ever day, but we must prepare for every outcome. If war cannot be avoided, well-trained men will have the best chance of survival, and bringing war to a swift conclusion. If I can do anything to limit the misery of loss among the families of my men, I will.'

'There must be much to do, not least training them in weaponry. Have many fired a musket before?'

'No, and we are increasing our supply of guns, but we haven't completely abandoned the old ways. Many will be armed with pikes and we also have a small contingent of archers.' Skippon twisted in his saddle and pointed. 'If you look to north edge of the field you will see a group practicing in the butts.'

'But why? Surely the bow has been replaced by muskets and pistols?'

'Not completely. Archers still have many advantages. They are silent, accurate, and reliable. Arrows can be fired more rapidly and, with care, can be used in wet weather when gunpowder is damp. They can also carry messages. I would take more archers if it were possible. But, sadly, it is now a scarce skill.

'You can train a musketeer in five days. You cannot develop an effective archer in five years. It takes decades to build the strength to draw a bow, something they learn from childhood. Many of our recruits are from London and have never picked up a bow in their life. That ability is lost to them, forever. But while we have recruits from the fields of Essex and Kent, we will make good use of their skills.'

Tom thought of his apprentice bookkeeper Sam, a farmer's son from Berkshire. He had kept his bow when he moved to London and occasionally practiced on these same butts on Finsbury Field. He said he didn't want to lose the power to draw a bowstring. Tom knew Sam would welcome the chance to join fellow archers.

'Well, I mustn't take up more of your time. This meeting has been most instructive.'

'It is the least I can do, given the assistance you are providing to Mr. Pym.'But before you go, may I ask, do you have experience of military life?'

'No. I am a merchant by trade. Any action I have seen has been limited to fighting storms and keeping order on board ship.'

'So you are used to giving orders and instilling discipline.'

'We cannot sail without it.'

'Well, if you believe the rights of Parliament and the people should be protected, a man of your experience would be most welcome to our cause. We need more officers of the right calibre, given our expansion. The King's navy has surrendered to Parliament, so we now possess almost all his ships. There is little for them to do other than keep the Thames open for shipping, and transport supplies to the ports in our control across the country. No, I think your talents, if you'll excuse my use of the word, would be better devoted to our endeavour on land, if you have a mind to do so. Pray, tell me more of your experience.'

Tom explained the Tallant's merchant business and the part he played within it, including his first trading visit to India, three years ago, to buy spices for the London market.

'And you were the captain?'

'The voyage required an experienced, seafaring skipper, but I was in overall charge, responsible for our safe return.'

Skippon paused as a column of men marched past, kept in step by a raw-throated sergeant. 'As you can see, I have plenty of eager recruits, thank the Lord. But I am short of experienced officers, especially now, given recent events.'

There was another, longer, pause.

'Recent events?'

Skippon said nothing. Tom saw he was weighing up whether to share his information. 'Well if you are to join us as an officer, it is only right you know. We are expanding the number of brigades to accommodate the surge in recruitment, so we were looking for more officers, but now we have even more to find. Two of my brigade commanders have died…have been killed…in unusual yet identical circumstances in the last fortnight.'

'How? What were the circumstances?'

'Hard to explain really. Both were travelling on horseback, on separate days, through the London streets when they were shot.'

'Were there many people in the streets at the times of the killings?'

'Yes. In both cases the streets were full when the men were shot but nobody witnessed the attack or saw anyone fire a weapon.'

'Did these attacks have anything else in common?'

'Not really. Only that the two men were both travelling to Finsbury to oversee training and both attacks took place within the City walls, on Coleman Street, but on different days.'

Tom tried to picture the killings. The assassin had to be close to his victim to make a single killing shot, with a weapon he could hide until the last minute, such as a pistol. In addition, he required a street busy with people, to let him slip into the crowds and escape. But, if so, how could shooting someone from close range, while surrounded by people, go unnoticed?

'It has presented me with a dilemma,' Skippon continued. 'The obvious solution would be to tell our commanders in future to make their way to Finsbury Fields by a different route. But what's to stop the assassin following them down these side streets and shooting them wherever he chose?

'In addition, Coleman Street is a strong centre of support for Mr. Pym, so he prefers the commanders to ride to Finsbury on this route, to raise morale among the citizens. They often arrive at the fields with half a dozen new recruits tagging along. It would raise questions if they suddenly took more circuitous routes, skulking in side streets, afraid of their own shadow. On the other hand, I cannot afford to lose my experienced commanders at this rate. It is a damnable nuisance.

'So I am in the process of promoting several of my troop leaders to brigade commanders, which has created vacancies at the troop level. You have experience of commanding men, albeit in different circumstances. I can offer you a post as leader of a troop, if the current survival rate of our commanders does not put you off? What do you think?'

Tom was taken aback. He liked Skippon but was still uncertain about where his support lay in the growing crisis. He wasn't ready for such a commitment. 'Commander Skippon, I'm not sure I am worthy of such responsibility. Let me reflect upon it. However I am more certain about the abilities of another, to investigate your troublesome killings, and I will request their assistance.'

Chapter 8

Cheapside

Outside the light was fading. He felt his way down the cellar steps, his single candle casting a pale shadow on the ceiling.

When he reached the bottom, he walked to a corner of the cellar and moved a pile of rough cotton sacks. Underneath was the top half of an old oak door, which he carefully lifted and leaned against the nearby wall.

He placed the candle on the stone floor and searched his pocket. His fingers found two more stub ends with charred wicks, which he lit from the flame of the first and placed next to it.

He picked up each candle and, sinking to his knees, placed them in three corners of the floor now revealed in the corner. He studied the cobbles for scratches and grunted in satisfaction. Relaxing, he retrieved a long, thin-bladed knife from his pocket and carefully prised the edge of one of the cobbles from the floor, humming as he set about his work.

A dog was barking. Where? Why? He paused and waited, cobble in hand. The dog barked again, this time with more urgency. He cursed his carelessness, making too much noise. He would not move until it stopped, however long that took. Last week he was immobile for a quarter of the hour when he heard voices outside in the street. He was good at this. He had the patience. Nothing on earth was more important than keeping his secret safe.

Silence returned and he set to work again. Methodically he removed five more cobbles to reveal rough soil underneath. He pulled a cloth from his pocket, which he unfolded and placed to his left. He then used his knife to scrape away the soil. A metallic scrape told him he had found what he was looking for and he continued to push the soil to the sides of the hole in the floor.

'Not long now, my lovelies. I have some new friends for you.'

He worked methodically until the top of a large metal box was revealed. Placing the knife on the floor, he leant forward and gripped its two handles. Again he stopped to listen, then with a grunt, hauled it out of the ground and placed it carefully on the cloth.

Brushing the dirt from its front, he inserted a key and turned. The well-oiled lock yielded effortlessly and he sat back on his haunches, savouring the moment. Moving the candles closer, he opened the lid to reveal a velvet-lined tray which he placed on the floor. Underneath, the box was full of small velvet bags of different sizes.

He reached inside his shirt for a leather pouch held around his neck. Picking up the velvet tray, he carefully poured out the contents of the pouch. Flashes of vivid blue and soft green were caught in the candlelight as two sets of earrings tumbled in a heap onto the tray. He gently untangled the jewellery and examined it closely, turning it over. Both sets had a similar design, the stones held like tiny bunches of grapes in a falling framework of gold and white enamel. One was in lapis, the other emeralds. Both were exquisite.

He murmured his approval as he laid the jewels across his palm and watched the reflected candlelight dance in his hand. The emeralds were particularly fine, unusually pale yet lustrous. He searched inside the open box and found an empty velvet bag, which he opened carefully and slipped the earrings inside. This was placed with the other bags and he paused before replacing the tray. With the container uncovered and open, he desperately needed to enjoy some of his finer specimens while they were available. Just to have them under his care and protection, glistening in his hands, was enough to improve his humour and dispel the gloom that cast a shadow over his life these days. The emerald parrot perhaps, or the superb scent bottle, adorned with diamonds, opals, rubies and pink sapphires, one of his favourites. But he had insufficient time. Another appointment was approaching and he required fifteen minutes precisely to return everything to its place, in a way that would look as though nothing had been disturbed, then leave his hiding place using the secret passage.

If he rushed it, he would not sleep that night for worry. He knew that for a fact.

Chapter 9

Coleman Street, London

The trooper strode in front of Tom and Elizabeth, surveying the surrounding houses. He stopped, took a step to one side, gazed up and down the street and nodded.

'This be it. This is where Captain Hudson was shot.'

Tom examined the ground for signs of blood but the muddy surface had been churned by dozens of cartwheels. 'How can you be so sure?'

'Because I ran into the tavern opposite for a cloth to stop the bleeding, but it did no good.'

Tom glanced at the sign swinging outside the inn. The Moon and Stars. Perhaps a good omen, given Elizabeth's knowledge of astronomy?

They were standing on Coleman Street, a main route to Moorgate, one of the guarded gateways in the old city wall. It was nearing midday and the street was thronged with traders, hawkers, beggars and thieves – a typical London thoroughfare. Elizabeth had been reluctant at first to help Skippon find the killer. She was preoccupied with solving the jewel thefts and helping William Harvey. But her natural curiosity won her over when Tom explained the circumstances, as he hoped, no knew, it would.

She approached the trooper. 'I have questions to ask and it is vital you answer them as accurately as possible.'

The man looked anxious. 'I'll do my best ma'am, but it happened so quick.'

'How many of you were travelling with Captain Hudson?

'Four of us, as his escort.'

'Were you on horseback?'

'No, only the captain. We walked alongside.'

'Alongside? Not behind or in front.'

'Hard to remember exactly…' Elizabeth gave the trooper a hard stare. 'Err, let me think again,' he said 'Yes. I think one of us was on either side, with two at the back. I was on the captain's right hand side.'

'What time of the day was it?'

'A couple of hours earlier than today.'

'What was the weather like?'

'The weather? I don't recall, ma'am. Nothing I can remember.'

'So neither pelting with rain nor burning hot? A bit like today? Cloudy?'

'Well, when you put it that way, it must have been because I would have remembered otherwise, wouldn't I?'

'Was it as busy as this?'

'Busier, I would say. A lot of the lads were heading to Finsbury Fields for drill practice.'

'Ah…so more people were heading in your direction, out of London, than coming in?'

'Yes.'

'So you reached this point. Describe what happened next.'

The man looked awkward. 'Well, there's not much to say. We were walking along and suddenly the captain shouted out and fell from his horse. I tried to revive him but he was dead within minutes.'

'So you didn't see anyone near you with a gun. Or hear a shot?'

'No ma'am. It was noisy in the street, with the people coming and going. And no one other than us took any notice of the captain's fall, so no alarm was sounded. Everyone kept walking along normal-like. I would have spotted anyone running away.'

Elizabeth lifted her head and carefully turned full circle, examining the houses that lined the route, leaning over the street below. 'Thank you. That is all. You have been most helpful.'

The trooper glanced at Tom questioningly. He nodded to the man who looked relieved and strode away towards Moorgate.

'Can you draw any conclusions from his account.'

'Possibly. I need to wait until the next time to be more certain.'

'The *next* time? You think there will be more.'

'Why not? The assassin has been successful twice. His actions are hindering Parliament's defence of London. Skippon might flood Coleman Street with troops to improve security but, after days of waiting, vigilance would drop, leaving the killer to strike again whenever he chose.

'So, how does he do it?'

'There are a number of possible explanations but I cannot make any deductions without a vital piece of missing information. And for that I will need to examine the next victim immediately after his death. It is essential, Tom. I must be told as soon as it happens. But, first, I require the help of Sam.'

Tom was chilled at the thought of another soldier, currently alive and well, dying when their knowledge might prevent it. But this assassin must be stopped, even if it meant sacrificing another life. Not for a moment did he question Elizabeth's ability to make use of the poor unfortunate's death to bring the killer to justice. But it was hard to stop pondering her matter-of-fact acceptance of what was required. Yet again, it was a rational response, which unnerved and impressed him in equal measure.

Riding away, he reflected on her decisiveness in pursuit of Skippon's cause and realised what he must do.

Chapter 10

The Tallant warehouse

'You've done *what?*'

Ralph Tallant stared at his son in disbelief. He had been tending the fire in the parlour when Tom entered. Now he stood up, a piece of sea coal in his hand, his mouth agape. 'What were you thinking? What about the business? Who will run the warehouse?'

'That is why I have chosen the Trained Bands, father. Their purpose is to defend London so I will remain here and manage my work around my new duties. I did the same when I was regularly attending Parliament but now it is half empty. Many of the King's supporters like Barty have left. I see little point in remaining there when I can use that time more profitably.'

'I cannot agree, Thomas. Now is *exactly* the time to be there, to keep an eye on Pym's latest follies.'

'I have contacts who can do that.'

Ralph shook his head and threw the coal onto the fire, reaching for a rag to wipe his hands. 'It's not the same. And what about our customers in the Exchange? What will they think, if they support the King, buying pepper from one of Pym's men?'

'Please father. Listen to me. I know you and other merchants are avoiding taking sides but lines are being drawn and it will soon be impossible to isolate yourself from events. What would have happened if the King had kept control of the navy? You said he would blockade the Thames to stop supplies reaching the Parliamentary forces gathering here in the capitol. That would have been the end of all trading for the Tallants. Can't you see we will have no control over our destiny until this dispute is resolved, but we must protect ourselves until it blows over? I'm best placed to do that with the Trained Bands, based here in London, where I can keep an eye on Sam and Andrew, who have both enrolled.'

'In God's name,' Ralph exclaimed. 'So that leaves Isaac to run the warehouse! Perhaps we should ask your mother and Ellen to unload the spice when our next shipment arrives!'

'We are not the only ones in this situation,' Tom retorted. Parliament has declared apprentices can join the Trained Bands and not endanger their indentures. The tide is running against you. You can't stop Sam and Andrew enrolling if they wish to. I agree about its impact on our trading in the Royal Exchange. The best solution there is for you take that responsibility back, until the current difficulty has been resolved.'

'Current difficulty? You make it sound like we've broken a cartwheel on the wharf. This 'difficulty' may go on for months. How do expect me and Isaac to manage for that length of time? Really Tom, this is too much. To make such a decision without asking me first. I don't know what's got into you,' and, throwing the rag on the floor, Ralph stormed from the room.

Tom frowned. He had expected his father's displeasure but his reaction had been ridiculous. He could hire additional men to handle cargo in the warehouse and he, Tom, would be there for much of the time. No, this was more about his father losing control, a situation Tom knew he would both loathe and, in truth, fear.

'What's the matter with your father, Tom?' It was Elizabeth. Tom had forgotten they had agreed to meet to take a boat on the river. 'He passed me on the path down to the warehouse and barely offered a greeting, not like him at all.'

Tom hesitated. He hadn't yet told Elizabeth about his decision to join Skippon's men and did not know how she would react. 'I have given him news which I now wish to share with you.'

Elizabeth said nothing but looked a little apprehensive. She reached for her pipe and tobacco.

'I have agreed to join the Trained Bands under the command of Philip Skippon.'

'Oh, I see. And why is that?'

It was a simple question without an easy answer. So Tom explained his reasoning to Elizabeth who listened carefully while she filled and lit her pipe. Finally she spoke.

'I understand and would have expected your desire to protect, because that is you, Tom. It is instinctive. My instinct is to abhor any fighting, No good comes from it - only human suffering. However, if you are to take up arms, it is better to defend, not attack. And, of course, I am comforted that you will remain in London,' and at this she lent over and embraced Tom, holding him tight. She pulled back and held his gaze with her deep brown eyes. 'However I have a sense, which I can't dismiss, that this conflict will neither be short or confined to London. You must pray I am wrong.'

Tom heard voices at the front of the warehouse and Isaac entered the room, looking worried. 'Two soldiers to see you, Master. Shall I let them come through?'

'Of course, Isaac.' and he turned to the door as two uniformed men entered. The leading man stepped forward, removing a leather glove and proffering his hand. 'I am pleased to meet you, Mr. Tallant. My name is Sergeant Henry Appleyard and I am here on the orders of Philip Skippon, commander of the London Trained Bands.'

Tom glanced at Isaac who looked aghast.

'Myself and Trooper White,' and he nodded towards the other man, 'are here to help you in the matter discussed with Mr. John Pym. Commander Skippon has told me to offer you every assistance in your task.'

Isaac was starting to shake and slowly sat down in a chair.

'As I am here on urgent official business, perhaps we can find a more private place, Mr. Tallant, to continue our discussion?'

Chapter 11

The Moon and Stars tavern, Coleman Street

Elizabeth paused at the entrance to the back room at the Moon and Stars tavern.

Less than an hour ago, she had been sitting in her study when a message arrived from Tom. The killer had struck again. She grabbed her bag and left within minutes. It was only now, as she was about to see the victim, that she worried about his sacrifice. Would it be in vain? Once again, the thought they might have prevented this man's death flashed through her mind. 'Stop this way of thinking. No good will come of it', and taking a deep breath she pushed the door open.

Tom had arrived and was leaning over a body on a rough wooden table. Two soldiers were standing in the corner. Tom glanced over and nodded to Elizabeth who took off her coat and undid her bag. She took out a large white apron, slipped it over her head and knotted the ties behind her back. Tom watched her lay out the contents of her bag: a wet cloth, a narrow length of wood, paper and a piece of red chalk. Finally she rolled up her sleeves and approached the body. Elizabeth picked up the man's arm, flexed it at the elbow and pressed his skin.

'Tom. Please take off his jacket and shirt and roll him on his side. Have you spoken to these men?' she said, looking towards the troopers.

Tom nodded as he carefully removed the victim's coat. 'Sounds much like the previous case. They were walking with their commander when he toppled from his horse, wounded. They didn't hear or see any shot or shooter.'

'And this occurred recently?'

'Near two hours ago.'

'Then we do not have a moment to lose.'

Despite the urgency, she noticed how Tom rolled the man over, handling him with care and dignity. 'Have I turned him far enough?'

'No, a little further. I need clear access to the wound.' The man was now on his side, lying on his left shoulder. 'Hold him there, please Tom. I need to see both his front and back at the same time.' She examined the body closely. 'Hmm, that's interesting.' The man had two wounds, one at the top of his chest, to the left of his throat, and the other in his upper back, to the right of his spine.

Elizabeth used the wet cloth to clean away the caked blood revealing a neat hole in his chest and a larger, ragged tear in his back. She picked up the piece of wood laid out on the table. It was a slender arrow shaft, without iron tip or feathered flights. A narrow length of willow, sharpened to a point at one end. 'Now, Tom. I need you to hold his shoulders firmly from the back while I stand in front of him.'

The two troopers in the corner stirred and started murmuring to each other.

'Quiet there!' Tom shouted as he watched Elizabeth lift one end of the arrow shaft and position it in the neat hole in the man's chest. She carefully worked the willow into the hole, applying increasing amounts of pressure, and twisting the shaft slowly in her fingers.

'Hold this for a moment, please Tom' and she offered the arrow shaft to Tom. 'Hold his right shoulder and use your other hand to hold the shaft steady. On no account let it fall out of the wound,' and she changed her position to look at the victim side on. 'Now please tilt the shaft upwards a little. That's enough! Hold it there.' Elizabeth returned to her position in front of the victim and took over from Tom, holding the piece of willow. 'I now need to push harder, so hold him firmly.'

She lent over the man and attempted to push the shaft further into his body, which at first resisted. She grunted with effort, tilted the arrow a little higher, and the shaft jerked forward by an inch. She reduced the pressure and twisted the wood while continuing to push. The arrow was now moving more steadily and within seconds its tip emerged from the middle of his back. She pushed again until it protruded by two or three inches.

Elizabeth stopped and released the arrow shaft. She wiped her brow with the edge of her apron and stood back. 'Good heavens, it worked!' she gasped under her breath and studied the body carefully. 'Tom, we now need to sit our friend up. There should be enough flexibility in his body. Bend him into a sitting position while he's lying of his side and then we'll pull him upwards, so he's sitting up.'

The officer was not a large man and they soon had him in position, his legs along the table and his torso upright, supported by Tom. 'Can you lift his chin off his chest, I need him sitting as upright as possible. This part is critical. Yes, that's much better. Now keep him absolutely still.'

Elizabeth picked up the piece of red chalk and paper. She studied the strange sight, the willow shaft sticking out of his back and chest. It reminded her of Bonsignori's painting of Saint Sebastian pierced by arrows. She worked quickly, drawing the side of the man's torso, paying particular attention to the arrow's entrance and exit in relation to the rest of his upper body.

Tom's arms were starting to ache. 'I'm not sure how much longer I can keep him still,' he called to Elizabeth.

'You must, for one more minute,' she replied, her voice detached, yet urgent. Elizabeth bent down on her haunches. She lowered her head until her eyes were level with the table and held the paper in front to her. With her other hand she drew a short line across the bottom of the paper representing the table top. She then ran quickly to the front and back of the man, checking the position and angle of the arrow's entry and exit points. Satisfied, she stepped back. 'You can lower him now, Tom.'

Tom lowered the officer back on to his side, as Elizabeth gently withdrew the arrow shaft. She rolled him on his back and studied his face for the first time. Younger than she expected, his skin was drained of colour, his brow smooth, his expression peaceful. Her work done, her doubts once more clouded her conscience and she caught her breath. She took hold of his cold arm. 'What have we done, young sir, to deny you of life, so that others may live?'

Tom opened his mouth to speak but thought better of it. He knew the weight of responsibility on Elizabeth's shoulders. She now had to deduce how the assassin attacked, and stop him, to justify this young man's death. He did not envy her.

Chapter 12

Fetter Lane, Holborn

Elizabeth entered the room and surveyed the wreckage. She cast her mind back to William Harvey's lodgings. As she moved forward, shards of glass from a broken window cracked beneath her feet, and Robert Cooke turned from his examination of a strong box, on its side on the floor.

'Ah Miss Seymour. I'm glad you received my message. You wished to be told of any other raids…' and he paused and looked around the room. 'Nothing has been touched, as you requested.'

'Thank you Mr. Cooke. I appreciate the owner will wish to make the building secure as soon as possible, so I will not be long.'

'He and his wife are both away this week. Former clients of mine… I have taken it upon myself to repair the damage in their absence. So please, look where you wish.'

'The house was empty when the robbers struck?'

'Alas no. One servant had remained to look after the property. He has been badly beaten and now cared for by a relative.'

'Can I question him?'

'Not at present. I am told he is barely conscious and may not survive the day.'

'So they are prepared to kill for their prize, it seems.'

Cooke was silent, but Elizabeth felt his anger building. 'This is the ugly side of my business, Miss Seymour. Precious stones are God's bounty, the greatest fruits of His world. Some appreciate them and wish to share their beauty. But they bring out the worst in others. I have seen this before, the harm their greed can inflict, but it is now becoming commonplace. It is a sign of the wicked times we are living in. These attacks will only get worse, I am sure of it.'

'Why is that, Mr. Cooke?'

'Because our world is turned upside down. Look at this room. It is the work of a mob. Everything has been taken, cleaned out. There is no finesse; no understanding of what is valuable and what is not. It is literally pearls before swine. In the past, jewel theft was by sleight of hand or a silent thief in the night. Now they don't care. Why pick a lock when you can smash it? But what can you expect when our King has been chased out of his own capital. There is no respect any more. Not even for their own kind!'

'What do you mean?'

'The louts responsible for this are the same people who are baying for the King's blood. But the family living here are honest Protestants, distant relatives of the Earl of Essex, who presently commands the Parliamentary army. It makes no sense.

'And what are they doing with their booty? Since our first meeting, I have kept a close eye on the market in London, looking for jewels up for sale from the recent thefts. I have not seen a single ring, brooch or pair of earrings. What is the point of stealing all this wealth if you're not going to sell it? Like most else these days, it makes no sense at all!'

Robert Cooke realised the room was now echoing to his strident voice and stopped. He took a moment to compose himself. 'Forgive me, Miss Seymour. I will cease, as you require time to observe the room. But to see my country, England, descending into barbaric chaos, is a bitter pill to swallow.' Cooke was close to tears and Elizabeth felt sorry for him – one of many swept along by current events, taken from the world they knew and loved.

She moved to the broken window and carefully peered through. Other than a few small pieces, no glass was visible on the ground outside. It overlooked the house's private rear garden, which could be entered by a side alley from the front street, a perfect place to break in unnoticed. She examined the frame. Most of the glass had been removed and no leading was evident. She looked at the distribution of the shattered glass in the room. She picked up two pieces, one from directly below the window and another from the middle of the room, and compared their size and shape.

She bent down and touched a dark stain on the floorboards. It stuck to her finger. Congealed blood. 'Was this where the servant was found?'

Cooke nodded. 'Yes, poor man.'

Elizabeth examined the upended strong box. The lock was intact and closed, as were the iron bands reinforcing its curved lid and sides. Overlaying metal plates also protected the hinges. It was a formidable obstacle, which must have cost the owners a considerable sum. But it had one weakness that Elizabeth wagered the thieves had known all about.

She turned the trunk over. Its base had been smashed apart. She bent down and tapped some of the splintered wood around the gaping hole. It was thinner and with no protective iron banding. At first sight, the strong box was an imposing barrier, but the 'back door' to the vault had been weak, a fatal economy by the makers. She stood up and brushed the creases out of her dress. 'Thank you Mr. Cooke. I have seen all I need. A description of the missing jewels would be helpful when the owners return.'

Elizabeth sat in her carriage slowly wending its way towards Moorgate and the road home to Clerkenwell. She pondered on what she had witnessed and frowned. It was now possible to add another piece of information about the thieves she was seeking. They were not only brutal but also experienced. They had known at a glance that the way in to that safety box was through the bottom. There was not a scratch on the large lock.

And where were these jewels going? If not this country, perhaps overseas? And then a thought occurred - one person would might need jewels to sell abroad. Her old adversary Henry Jermyn was currently with the Queen in The Hague, attempting to raise funds for the King's army. It would be just his style to organise these brutal robberies to fill his coffers.

She had to find out if this was a possibility. The quickest way to Jermyn was through Lucy, the two people in the world she did not want to be indebted to; but there was no avoiding it.

Chapter 13

The Tallant warehouse

Tom raked the embers of the sea coal in the parlour fireplace and added more fuel. It was a cold morning and he was meeting his father to discuss current spice stocks in the warehouse. Raised voices coming from the front room interrupted their conversation. Isaac was attempting to calm a visitor, but without success. Ralph and Tom strode from the parlour to be greeted by two familiar faces.

'Amos and Nathaniel. Greetings. What's amiss?'

'I'm sorry Master Ralph' Isaac stammered. 'I told the gentlemen we knew nothing about it, but they weren't having it.'

'Know about what, Isaac? What's the problem, Amos?'

The smaller man stepped towards Tom. He had a rotund figure, with a red face, topped with a black wig, slightly askew. 'The problem, Ralph, is your son Tom, or rather the soldiers he commands!'

Ralph shot a look at Tom who shrugged his shoulders. 'I have no idea what you are…'

'Well you should know what's going on in your own house, especially when it's damaging your neighbours' business.' At this, Nathaniel, the silent partner of the two, nodded his head vigorously.

Ralph looked perplexed. 'Amos. You, and Nathaniel have shared the wharf peacefully with Tallants for the last fifteen years or more. We're all merchants and merchants help their own. If one has been low on stock, the others have helped. If one urgently needed wharf space to unload, the others have tried to accommodate him.'

'So why has Tom turned our lives upside down in the last few days…him and his Sergeant Appleyard?'

Tom bowed his head in a moment of realisation. What has Appleyard been playing at? The timing of this news could not have been worse. 'Father, I can explain. I've been asked to search for contraband gunpowder which is to be shipped out of London to equip the King's army.'

Ralph Tallant's face held a cold fury, unnerving Tom. 'And you thought Amos and Nathaniel would be guilty of such a thing?'

'No! Well, I wouldn't have, but the search was conducted by Sergeant Appleyard, who has been assigned to assist me.'

'And who has wrecked our stores in the process,' Amos shouted. ' He made us empty the warehouse onto the wharf, while he searched inside. Kegs were split open, sacks pulled apart. All for us to clean up. And when we protested, he threatened to throw me in the Tower! And the same happened to Nathaniel.'

Tom took a deep breath. 'I can only apologise to you both and I will speak to Appleyard immediately. The matter is of the greatest importance and John Pym himself has ordered the search. Appleyard is determined to find the smugglers but clearly he has been over zealous in his search, and he will be told so...'

'But if you had informed me of this,' Ralph interrupted, 'I would have told you not to trouble Amos and Nathaniel. Nathaniel is a leading figure in Merchant Taylors, and Amos has donated to a school Nathaniel is founding through the Taylors to educate the poor. And, unlike me, they are both quiet, but active supporters of the Parliamentary cause. I cannot think of two less likely candidates on the wharf for such a misdeed.'

Tom blushed. He cursed Appleyard but, inwardly, knew it was his fault. He should have kept the sergeant on a tighter leash. He was aware that Appleyard was searching warehouses on the north bank, but had been distracted by other matters.

His father stepped forward. 'Gentleman. I was not aware of this and can only apologise on behalf of the Tallant family. I will make it my business to visit both your warehouses this week and offer reparations for any damage done to your stock, including direct replacement if we have the same available.' Tom winced. This would leave us short, something his father hated. The next few days would be difficult.

After further shaking of heads and grumbling, Amos and Nathaniel finally left, mollified by Ralph's offer and his continued assurances, as he personally showed them out, that such a thing would never happen again. Tom steeled himself as his father re-entered the room. Appleyard's mistake was exactly the consequence of taking sides that Ralph had predicted. He would not let Tom forget it. But his father simply walked up to him with a look of weary resignation.

'Father, about Amos and…'

'Forget it. They're a pair old women at the best of times. I'm sure the damage is not as bad as they say.' Tom thought of Appleyard's bullish manner and doubted that, but said nothing.

'I've been thinking on what you said, Tom. You're right, we'll have to get used to much worse in the months to come. And everyone will take a side, including you. No point in pretending otherwise.' Ralph took Tom by the shoulders, and stared into his eyes. The old steel had returned to his sapphire blue eyes.

'Just don't keep me in the dark, eh? For God's sake, don't keep me in the dark.'

Chapter 14

Coleman Street

Tom watched Philip Skippon stand by his horse checking the saddle straps and bridle. He had done this five minutes ago in the stable, a seasoned soldier's repeated ritual before confronting danger.

The commander of the Trained Bands handed the reins to his groom and knelt briefly by his horse to pray for the Lord's protection before stepping on to a mounting stool. With practised ease, he put his foot in the stirrup and swung his other leg over the broad back of his horse, the leather creaking as he settled in his saddle.

The early morning sun was bright in an azure, cloudless sky. The air was crisp, heralding the start of autumn. 'Come on, old girl. Let us see what this wonderful day has to bring us.' And he walked the horse towards the entrance to Coleman Street, accompanied by Tom on foot.

'Is all prepared?'

'Yes, sir. We have calculated where the assassin will be and have men ready to capture him as soon as he makes an appearance.'

'You're sure he will be there?'

'We cannot be certain but we've baited the trap with a prize he will find hard to resist.'

Skippon gave a hollow laugh. 'You mean me?'

Tom offered Skippon an apologetic smile. 'For days, we have been spreading the word in the taverns. The Commander of the Trained Bands will be riding up Coleman Street to Finsbury Fields this morning. I am most grateful you have agreed to this, Commander. It's imperative to catch this killer before he does any more harm and I do not know of a better way to tempt him into action.'

Tom had been worried by Elizabeth's suggestion to use Skippon. He knew his commander would agree, but it would be a disaster if he was injured or worse, and the recriminations didn't bear thinking about.

'So the plan is I ride up Coleman Street, accompanied by a small number of men on foot?'

'Yes, exactly as the previous victims did.'

'And I can expect nothing to happen until we near the final stages of Coleman Street as it approaches the City Wall, close to Moorgate.'

'Exactly. One of my men Sam will be with the soldiers walking by your side, for added protection, but I will be some distance away, where we expect the assassin to be positioned.'

Skippon's horse stood placidly, unperturbed by the morning noise coming from the street in front of them. Exactly as we require, thought Tom. 'Let us get underway,' Skippon ordered. 'The sooner we start, the sooner this devil will be dancing from a rope.'

'Yes, sir. I will set off now and take up my position. You will follow in fifteen minutes, no sooner. Please keep to a steady pace and act as you would normally, stopping to talk to well-wishers or those wishing to enrol.

Skippon nodded and Tom set off for the end of Coleman Street. The road was filling rapidly with street traders, food shoppers as well as soldiers on their way to practice on Finsbury Fields. His chest tightened with apprehension as he approached his meeting place with Elizabeth. There was no turning back.

He found her on a street corner on the left of Coleman Street. She was peering out from a side alley and put her finger to her lips when she saw him. As he approached the alley, he noticed two of Skippon's personal guard, not in uniform, standing behind her, hidden from view. Tom looked back down Coleman Street. He estimated the Moon and Stars tavern was over two hundred yards away. 'Are you sure he will be here, where we stand? There's little cover and his target is too far away.'

'No he won't be here. He's up there.' and she pointed to the middle floor of large building next to them. 'If I am right, as I speak, the man we seek is sitting at a window on the corner of the first floor, looking down Coleman Street towards the Moon and Stars, waiting for his chance. You must trust the mathematics, Tom. My calculations are based on my examination. It's not possible that the previous shot was taken from anywhere *but* here.'

Tom studied the surrounding area. Walking from the tavern towards Moorgate, as Skippon would do, the street gradually widened until it neared its junction with the city walls. Here, a long building on the left jutted into Coleman Street, narrowing its width for the remainder of its length. The windows on the south side of this building offered a clear view back down the street to the oncoming Skippon. It was the perfect vantage point to kill the commander from fifty yards, but over two hundred? Surely, it was impossible.

'There is no time for further explanations. We must be ready, as soon as Skippon appears. I visited this house yesterday. It is a mixture of businesses and lodgings. I have secured a room near to the killer's vantage point. Let us go there quietly now' and she ushered Tom and the two troopers inside.

They walked carefully up a flight of wooden steps. Each creaked alarmingly under their weight and again Elizabeth signalled for silence. They reached the first floor and turned right along a narrow corridor. A shaft of sunlight lit the passage from the first door on the left, which was slightly ajar. Elizabeth paused, listening carefully, then tiptoed past, followed by the three others. Several yards further, she stopped to unlock the next door on the left and ushered them inside, closing the door quietly behind her.

The room was bare and the air smelt musty. Tom walked to the window and looked down the length of Coleman Street which, once again, was full of people as the Trained Bands headed to Finsbury Fields for drill practice. But, as yet, Skippon was nowhere to be seen.

'The assassin will be in that room,' she whispered, pointing to the left wall.

'The room we walked past?' Tom asked. 'Why don't we grab him now? He's left the door ajar.'

'Yes, that's strange. But we must catch him in the act, with all his concentration on his difficult kill. Walk in now and one of us would be dead within a second.'

'He's here, I can see Skippon!' Tom hissed. He stepped aside to let Elizabeth see though the window.

'He'll reach the Moon and Stars in a matter of minutes! Let me open the window, carefully now' and she reached forward to release the catch on the hinged casement. It swung outwards soundlessly. Elizabeth smiled at Tom. 'Liberal applications of pig fat yesterday have done their work, but I mustn't push it too far' and she tentatively leaned out to examine the window to her left. She pulled herself back in and whispered to Tom. 'It's open! But I don't expect to see the gun barrel as he won't want it to be visible from the street.'

Tom's pulse was quickening. Skippon was making steady progress towards the Moon and Stars. The commander remained beyond the killer's range, and they held their breath, watching Skippon stop and bend forward, talking to a boy in the crowd. He's got strong nerves, Tom thought appreciatively. I'd be rushing past the tavern, as soon as possible. Then he sensed Elizabeth's body tense as she looked first at Skippon and then back at the window on their left. She pulled her head back in, a startled expression on her face and ran out of the door, muttering 'no, no…how could I be so stupid!'

She turned right and ran quickly to the killer's hide, flinging the door open. Tom stifled a cry of alarm but when he entered, she was alone, the bright autumn sunlight illuminating the room. Over her shoulder, through the open window, Tom saw Skippon once again sitting upright in his saddle, moving forward. He was only yards from the tavern entrance. Elizabeth pushed past Tom. 'Wrong room. Follow me.' And she ran back into the corridor, returning left towards their hiding place, all attempt at subterfuge now abandoned.

He beckoned to the troopers who were standing bemused in the second room and they followed Elizabeth to a third door on her left. She paused and pointed to the lock. Tom quickly examined the door handle and stepped back. Leaning on the corridor wall opposite he took a deep breath and with a shout kicked the handle with the heel of his boot. The door flew open, Tom ran in and tripped over a body on the floor. A man was kneeling by the open window, his head crouched over the sights of a long musket pointed through the opening. He flinched slightly but didn't look up. Tom scrambled to his feet and threw himself at the gunman.

He crashed into the man, causing a sharp pain in his head and dancing stars in his eyes, then a loud roar and the smell of black powder and singed hair. Dazed, he put his hand to his face and saw it was covered with blood and black soot. He was aware of a struggle between the troopers and the assassin but as he feebly reached out a hand to help, blackness descended and he passed out.

Chapter 15

Philip Skippon's home, Moorgate

He awoke in an unfamiliar room, lying fully clothed on a bed. The sun was streaming through a small window. His head throbbed. Elizabeth sat in a chair next to him.

'Ah, my patient awakes,' she said with a smile and, leaning forward, kissed him tenderly on his left cheek. She paused to examine his face and reached for a pot of salve on a bedside table. She gently applied a little ointment to the right side of his face. 'You have a mild gunpowder burn. It will be sore for several days but should clear up.'

Tom lay on the bed, staring at the ceiling, attempting to clear his head. His memory returned and instantly he sat up, only to be hit by a wave of nausea.

'Skippon…?'

'Alive and unharmed. But the sign for the Moon and Stars now has a neat hole in it.'

'What happened…I must know.'

Elizabeth went to a bowl of water, squeezed out a cloth and, folding it, lay it across his brow. The cooling effect settled his mind. She sat on the edge of his bed and took hold of his hand. 'You stopped the assassin in time, despite a stupid mistake of mine. But let me start at the beginning,' and Elizabeth returned to her examination of the killer's previous victim. 'When I looked at his body, I was surprised to see an exit wound in his back. To kill in secret at close range, you need a small hand gun, hidden within a cloak. However, it is not possible for a pistol to generate enough force to shoot straight through a body, unless discharged point-blank. So, if that was the case, where were the powder burns on the young soldier?

'So a more powerful weapon must have been used, perhaps a musket. But from where?' Tom asked.

'Where, indeed? That was my problem. Could I solve the mystery with a little mathematics, using angles and distance? So I decided to conduct my investigation with the arrow shaft.' Tom was confused but knew better than to interrupt.

'William Harvey told me the flesh of a corpse remains supple and the wounds relatively open for several hours after death. That was why I had to know immediately the next victim was shot. And it worked far better than I dared hope. With a little effort, I was able to push the shaft through the passage created by the musket ball and out the other side. Then with your help, I made a record of the arrow's direction as it entered and left the body.

'Ah, the schets…'

Elizabeth looked puzzled. 'Schets?'

Tom looked at her in surprise. 'Sorry Elizabeth. That's Dutch for a rough drawing. What on earth am I saying? The bang on my head has rattled my brain.'

Elizabeth gave Tom a worried look and squeezed his hand. 'Tom, you should rest and I will complete my…'

'No, do continue. I must know.' She made an unconvincing play of reluctance but Tom was not fooled. Her face was animated with the realisation that her science had triumphed, and she was bursting to explain how.

'Well, if you insist…so, I took the drawing home and was able to work out the angle of the fatal musket ball as it approached and passed through the victim. One thing was immediately apparent. Although the victim was on horseback, the shot that killed him had been fired from above, down into his body.

'The next day, I returned to the Moon and Stars Tavern. I could see that buildings lined Coleman Street, either side of the fatal spot, but a shot from that position would have entered our victim's side. A face–on, front and back wound, such as his, would have been impossible from these positions.

'I walked along Coleman Street, from the tavern up to Moorgate, and counted out the yards until I reached the first building which *faced* the officer on horseback.'

'The one jutting into the street?'

' Yes. So, I went home and made a plan of the scene. If I was to get even a reasonably accurate result, I knew it had to work to scale, if possible. I did not possess any paper large enough, so I begged mama's indulgence and marked it out with chalk on our dining room table.

'I started by drawing a straight line along the table's length. I made a mark at the left end to signify the captain's position and measured out the rest of Coleman Street, heading towards Moorgate, converting every five yards into an inch on the plan. I then marked out the position of the most prominent buildings and, using the angle of entry into his upper chest, drew a rising line from the victim's position.

'I was concentrating deeply to keep the line straight, my face close to the table. This would indicate the musket ball's journey through the air, and it appeared to be continuing upwards forever. Out of the corner of my eye, I saw the end of the table approaching and my hopes began to fade. The musket ball looked certain to rise above the buildings. Clearly my experiment was flawed, unless an angel had descended from the heavens to shoot our unfortunate victim from the skies.

'Out of nowhere, an intersecting line of thin red chalk appeared in my side view. I paused to steady myself – my hand was aching with the effort of keeping the line straight

- and set off again, eventually reaching and cutting through this second line. I stopped, closed my eyes, said a prayer, and stood back from the table. I looked at the lines of red chalk. It had worked. The plan clearly showed the musket ball had been fired from a building.'

'The one jutting out? Where we found the killer?'

'Exactly. And, in addition, by measuring the distance from the intersection of the lines to the base of the building, I was able to establish which floor the shooter was on.'

Tom was astonished. He knew many examples of Elizabeth applying her scientific and mathematical knowledge to practical situations, but none quite like this. 'But how can you be sure it would be accurate. Your drawing of the body was only a rough sketch.'

'Yes, but I was only interested in the angle of the bullet's entry and exit points, as denoted by the arrow shafts, so I charted this as carefully as possible. I returned to Coleman Street to check my measurements. It could not have been any other building, even though it was two hundred yards away.'

Tom's elation and pride in Elizabeth's achievement was suddenly punctured. Her calculations had caught the killer but something was very wrong with her account. 'But Elizabeth…to hit a man accurately, if at all, with a musket shot from such a distance is extremely difficult. Once would be hard enough, but three times, and in the same part of the body on each occasion? Surely not.'

Elizabeth rose from the bed and, kneeling down, reached underneath. 'This will require both hands,' and she dragged out the longest musket he had ever seen and placed it on the bed next to him. Tom marvelled at its exquisite workmanship. It looked French, or perhaps German, with intricate decoration around the flintlock and along its extensive barrel.

Elizabeth picked up the musket. 'This was the killer's weapon, and look at this.' She pointed the firearm at Tom who instinctively flinched as he stared down its barrel. What a fearsome weapon. He examined the opening, running his finger around its edge.

'Rifling. I wouldn't have believed it would make such a difference.' He couldn't see far inside the barrel, but the evident craftsmanship told him the grooves spiralling down its interior would be perfectly aligned.

'How exactly does it work?' Elizabeth asked.

Tom turned the musket around and sighted down its enormous length. 'The barrels of most army muskets are smooth. When fired, the musket ball bounces inside the barrel and can fly out at an angle, making them inaccurate in battle. This is why they are usually fired at close range into a mass of men. This beauty is different. It's a hunting weapon. The rifling makes the musket ball spin as it travels inside the barrel, keeping it straight and extending its flight towards its target. You use a gun like this to fire at a single object, such as a deer. And they are effective from long distance, so you don't disturb your prey. Having said that, a shot requiring this level of accuracy over two hundred yards with any musket is a remarkable feat.'

'So why doesn't every musketeer in the army have these, if they are so accurate?'

'Because they are expensive to make, slower to load and the inside of the barrel needs frequent cleaning to avoid fouling with black power residue.'

'Well, thank goodness you jumped on him at the exact moment he fired. It was enough to make him miss and send his shot through the tavern sign.'

Tom puffed out his cheeks and exhaled slowly. His hand tentatively touched the burn on his cheek. 'And this?'

'From the ignition in the musket's firing pan, as he pulled the trigger. Your face was next to it as you landed on him.

The sound and smoke from the gunshot remained in the room, not heard by the people outside who were cheering and shouting. And for those next to Skippon, a brief flash from the barrel was not noticed from such a distance.'

Tom paused, taking it all in. The assassin's trap had been planned to the last detail. It was so good it had been set, again and again, without fear of discovery, until Elizabeth set her mind to unravelling it. 'I don't know if anyone other than you would have worked this out, Elizabeth. But you said you had made a stupid mistake?'

'Yes. One that almost cost Skippon his life. I built my plan around the information provided by the trooper who witnessed one of the killings. I calculated that, for the snare to be successful again and catch its victim, all the circumstances had to be the same, and indeed they were, except one.'

'Which was?'

'The weather, Tom. Today has been bright and sunny, not cloudy. And with the days getting shorter, the sun is lower in the sky. I knew something was wrong when I saw the door to the first room slightly ajar. It was not the kind of detail the killer would overlook.

'I was sitting by the window concentrating on Skippon's arrival but the image of the open door kept returning to my mind. What was it telling me? Then I realised. It wasn't the door; it was the sunlight shining through it. Intense, bright light. In a second I realised the gunman had been forced to move because the sun was blinding him. I looked around our room and noticed it was mostly in shade, cast by a tall house on Coleman Street near us. The killer would have tried to move here, before we arrived. But. of course the door was locked, and I had the key. So he chose the next room on our right, the third along the corridor, which was also in shade.'

'So that's why you ran out and led us to the next room.'

'Yes, I had no way of knowing for certain if he was there. Was he able to see Skippon clearly enough, from that angle, to take the shot? But I didn't have time to check.'

'And the man on the floor I tripped over…'

'…was the room's rightful occupant. He was only knocked out and thankfully is now recovering.'

Tom paused again to take it all in. It had been an extraordinary piece of quick thinking by Elizabeth. They were only seconds away from disaster.

'What about the killer? Who is he?'

'A gamekeeper for a lord in Berkshire, I think. He's claiming his employer supports the King and is the gun's owner, which makes sense. I don't think a gamekeeper would possess such an expensive weapon. He says his master planned the attacks and ordered him to embark on his killing spree. Threatened to eject him and his family from their estate cottage if he didn't.'

Tom looked again at the fine decoration on the stock. He thought of Philip Skippon, the son of a Norfolk gentleman. His father might own such a weapon for his country sport, the type of gun now used to attempt the murder of his son. The weight of the musket pressed down on him. In that moment, the stark reality of this object, its brooding and lethal menace, made him shudder. Their reasons may be many, often unclear; but his countrymen were set on destroying each other. Of that, he was no longer in any doubt.

Elizabeth left Tom to recover and sat exhausted in her father's carriage. The swaying motion as she travelled home soothed her agitated mind and she contemplated the day's events. It had been satisfying to foil the assassin with her mathematical knowledge but the episode had drained her. The death of the soldier, necessary to provide the information she required, still weighed heavily on her mind, but his sacrifice had stopped future deaths. Such logic would usually bring her solace, and it did again for a time. But it did not bring peace, and this unsettled Elizabeth, adding to her deepening unease.

Chapter 16

Cheapside

Elizabeth peered into the enveloping gloom. The early morning mist from the river was turning into fog, and seemingly thickening by the minute. She coughed in the damp air and tasted the sulphurous tang of coal smoke in the back of her throat. The fumes from the thousands of coal fires burning across London seemed to be trapped in the fog, forming a poisonous blanket over the city.

She'd received word from Lucy. She had heard from Henry Jermyn who denied all knowledge of acquiring further consignments of jewels to sell for the King's cause. Furthermore, he begged Lucy not to send any, if that's what she had in mind. It was proving difficult to get the right price for the Crown jewels and he did not want to distract buyers with other, no doubt inferior, gems. Elizabeth smiled. Typical Jermyn to assume that anything held by another would be inferior.

She was on her way to give Robert Cooke this latest information, but hadn't bargained on the fog. Her carriage came to a sudden halt. Ahead, two carts had collided in the murk, blocking the road. She was near to Cooke's workshop so decided to walk the last hundred yards.

Elizabeth carefully picked her way along Milk Street seeking solid, clean ground beneath her feet. Thankfully there had been no rain for a week, so the ever-present mud had dried, but the mounds of putrid rubbish still had to be negotiated. She sighed as she walked. What's wrong Lizzie, are you feeling tired? Should try reading less at night and sleeping more. But no, it wasn't that. She was weary. The investigation into Lucy's jewel was making little progress and the episode with the sniper had left her drained. Yes, they had caught the killer but it had been a close run thing and the image of her St. Sebastian, propped up on the tavern table, refused to leave her mind. Add to that the constant turmoil in her mind about the impending war and its choices and, with a start, she realised that she was not only weary. No, Elizabeth Seymour, who delighted in solving any problem thrown at her, was feeling overwhelmed.

She was pondering on this when a voice pulled her up short.

'Good morning. Miss Seymour.'

Elizabeth turned around, peering into the swirling mist.

'Who's there? Who is that?'

No reply. Elizabeth sensed the first prickle of alarm up her back. She slowly started moving forwards, then stopped again. A figure was emerging through the gloom, walking her way. She flinched and instinctively raised her arm to protect her face. It was a man, heading straight for her…until he saw her at the last minute and swerved aside with an apology.

Elizabeth didn't move as the passer-by disappeared into the fog.

'Now. Where's your manners, walking off when a gent greets you?'

That voice again. Now, even closer. She suddenly saw how vulnerable she was and, try as she might, her legs would not stop shaking. She must concentrate. Why did it sound familiar? Her instinct was to return to her carriage, but she needed to hear more, to recognise it.

'I say again, who are you, and what do you want?'

'It's what *you* want that matters, and never mind who I am.'

She listened carefully. It was a youthful voice, its expression hard but confident. This person was used to obedience and deference.

'I know you're off to visit your friend Mr. Cooke, and I know why.' The accent was from the river, almost exaggerated. Possibly Stepney? His knowledge of her was chilling. How long had she been followed and why had she not noticed anyone?

'I don't know what you are talking about.'

'Aaw, now don't be like that, sweetheart. Don't treat me like an idiot.' The voice was now filled with a weary, impatient menace. He knew she was at his mercy and disappointed she didn't seem to realise it. 'You've been sniffing around where you shouldn't, like a bitch on heat, haven't you? Poking around into matters that don't concern you. And that's got to stop, if you know what's good for you.'

'You mean the jewel theft at Fetter Lane?' Silence again.

Elizabeth didn't see the hand flash forward, out of the gloom, gripping her upper arm fiercely. She stifled a cry. Despite her terror, she knew her attacker intended to warn, not harm, her. Otherwise a silent blow to the back of her head would have sufficed. But if a cry alerted a passer-by, her attacker could be forced to violence.

The man was now closer, face-to-face. He was wearing a crude mask of sacking, with two eyeholes cut out. Swathed in fog, it radiated a horrifying menace. 'My message is simple. Stop what you're doing, while you still can. Understand?'

Elizabeth stared at the mask, trying to see the eyes within. Her resolve to keep this man in conversation was overwhelmed by an animal instinct for survival. Her legs started to buckle beneath her, and she could no longer speak.

The man held her up by his iron grip on her forearm and shook her furiously. 'Do you understand?' he hissed. Elizabeth nodded weakly, and in a moment her attacker let go and disappeared into the enveloping fog.

Elizabeth collapsed to the floor. She fought the hysteria inside. She must keep calm and remember what she had heard. Gradually her breathing eased and she got to her feet. It would be foolhardy to continue her journey to Robert Cooke now. She needed time and a quiet space to think.

She had heard that voice before. She was sure of it. But where?

Hours later, Elizabeth arrived at her parents' house, shaken and exhausted. Confronted by their front door, and the questions that lay behind it, she wanted to turn and flee into the night. To a field of soft grass which she could share with her star-lit companions, the constellations. They would soothe and calm her. But she didn't have the strength.

Eventually, bathed and refreshed, she was ready to face her parents and descended the stairs. A letter addressed to her in familiar handwriting had been left on the hall table.

It was from William Harvey. He was with the King's army at Worcester. There had been several skirmishes and his expectations had been proved correct. A number of the injured had gunpowder burns and he needed her advice. Could she be of assistance?

Chapter 17

The Tallant warehouse

The sluggish river eased past Tom as he stood on the wharf behind his warehouse. Another sharp shower peppered the water's surface, making him withdraw into the protection of his cloak. The weather matched his mood as he scanned the grey waters for signs of Jonah Dibdin.

It was five days since Elizabeth's note had arrived and she had rarely left his thoughts. What was she thinking of? A woman travelling through the English countryside in search of an advancing army! Tom had become used to Elizabeth's unconventional thirst for discovery. Indeed, it was one of the many things about her he loved. But this was madness.

When he received her letter, he rode to her parent's home to see if it was true. Her mother and father were accustomed to her wild spirit, but they too were aghast at this latest escapade. Forbidding her would have been useless – she would have left anyway under cover of dark- so they persuaded Elizabeth to take a servant and both had departed on horseback a few hours later.

Tom was worried about Elizabeth but also missed her powers of deduction. The more he knew Philip Skippon, the more he wanted to bring him a victory and capture the gunpowder intended for the Royalist cause. It would be a large shipment, requiring a proper wharf and dock to load a vessel which would be too tall to pass under London Bridge. So they concentrated on quaysides east of the bridge, on the north and south side of the Thames. His search so far had been fruitless, despite Sergeant Appleyard's zeal, and with each passing day he dreaded news that the powder had slipped through his fingers. He was running out of ideas and getting desperate when he received a message that Jonah wanted to meet him.

The showers abated, replaced by a stinging wind blowing up the river from the cold expanse of the Thames estuary. 'Surprised to find a merchant gentleman away from his warm fire indoors.'

Tom jumped at the sound of the familiar voice and spun round. 'Jonah! How did you get there?'

'Because, while you kept looking forward like you were on deck at sea, I was slipping along the north bank of the river, hugging the quayside. Easy as wink to fool you,' and he gave Tom a mirthless grin, revealing the latest gap in his front teeth.

Tom was not in the mood for Jonah's sardonic humour. 'Well that's very clever, Jonah. But what is your news?'

The waterman put on his best injured face. 'Well, thank you so much! I set out on this inclement morning, to provide you with the information you seek, when I might have been warming my hands with me mates around the brazier at Wapping Stairs…'

'All right,' Tom hissed in exasperation. 'I am sorry, Jonah. You have not found me in a good temper. Now, your news?'

Jonah sniffed and composed himself. 'Well, I wanted to make my point, that's all.'

The man was talking in riddles. Tom took a deep breath, keeping his voice calm. 'What do you mean, Jonah? What 'point'?'

'Word on the wharf is you're looking for a certain cargo.'

Tom was about to say 'How do you know?' then realised how foolish that would sound. Of course Jonah knew, when Appleyard's searches had been so heavy-handed. The waterman's tendency to gossip was why Tom had not included him in the search in the first place. He wanted as few people as possible to know about his mission. But, thanks to Appleyard, this was now impossible.

'So what did you want to tell me, Jonah?'

'That you'll never find this shipment, the way you are going about it.'

'And what has creeping up on me got to do with that?'

'I've been hearing grumbles all along the north and south side. This jumped-up merchant turning businesses upside down, accusing honest men of smuggling gunpowder and letting his soldiers wreck their warehouses.'

Tom frowned. 'They'll soon get over it. What else can I do?'

'Spread your gaze, as you should have done with me. You didn't spot me until I was under your nose, because I wasn't in the place you expected me to be, out in the middle.'

Tom's irritation was rising once more. 'But we know the size of wharf they require to load such a cargo, and we've been looking there.'

The rain started to hammer down again, bouncing off the wharf boards where Tom stood. 'Come, Jonah. This game of 'All Hid' you're enjoying will clearly take a while longer. Let us at least keep dry and warm. Stow your oars and come inside.'

They moved in to the warehouse. Dibdin settled by the parlour fire while Tom removed his dripping cloak and brought them two mugs of beer. Jonah drained his in one draught. 'That's a nice drop, very nice.'

'Now please get to the point, Jonah. What's on your mind?'

'You're looking in the wrong place.'

'So you say, but how can we consider elsewhere, given their requirements.'

'Because they will have done, when they planned this. Anyone with a pinch of sense would know the main docks east of the bridge would be first searched if word got out. So they needed somewhere else, more private.'

'But where else is available?'

'Their second problem. You've searched the big docks. So they would have to use something smaller.'

'But how would that work?'

'Their third problem. To use a smaller quay, they would have to load up a different way.'

'But it would attract attention if they were rowing the gunpowder out, one barrel at a time. They would surely be spotted.'

'Unless they chose somewhere quiet and close to a wharf which would take something bigger than a wherry.'

'But where would they find such a place?'

'How well do you know the river?'

'Very well, of course. I spend all my time here down at the warehouse.'

'Yes, but when was the last time you rode along its length, north and south, and seen how quickly the city is spreading along its banks.'

Tom paused. He had thought about this only a few weeks ago. How these days, as the Tallant business grew, his world was shrinking to the warehouse and the Royal Exchange, with a beaten path between.

'Have you been to Wapping, Stepney or Poplar lately? You can go to bed one night and wake up the next day to a new quayside and warehouses. Not as big as around here, but they're nice and quiet, and you can berth more than a row boat.'

The light of dawning realisation lit Tom's features. 'Well at least it gives somewhere different to look. Thank you Jonah. It's worth a try.'

"It's worth more than that. While your soldier boys have been rampaging like a couple of young bulls up and down north wharf, I've been quietly rooting around elsewhere, and I've picked up word of something afoot near the Isle of Dogs. I'd place a few pennies it's your precious gunpowder, if I was a betting man which of course I ain't', and Jonah's knowing grin returned.

'Can you take me there?'

'For a fee, I'll take you anywhere.'

'Right, meet me back here in two hours. I'll bring Sam with me.'

Tom smiled as the boatman walked out of the warehouse. Clearly, Elizabeth was not alone in her powers of deduction. He was surrounded by deep thinkers.

Tom called for his horse Meg and set off for the firing butts on Finsbury Fields. The air crackled with musket fire, the acrid smell of burnt gunpowder drifting on the breeze. He spotted Sam drawing his bow, steadying his aim, and stifled his call of welcome. Never disturb an archer when he's about to release. A slight movement could send the bolt anywhere. Tom waited until the arrow hit its target with a satisfying 'thunk' and Sam lowered his bow.

'Sam! Over here!' he yelled as Meg trotted towards him. He saw two other men heading in their direction. Good. Sergeant Appleyard had received his message. 'Thank you for coming at short notice. I have welcome news…'

'If it's about the gunpowder shipment, I think we are close to a discovery,' Appleyard interrupted. 'White and I have returned from Southwark, where we picked up a strong tip in one of the stews.'

'That's good to hear, sergeant, and I thank you for your continued diligence. But I believe we must seek pastures new, and stop ploughing the same furrow.'

Appleyard's brow creased. 'But this is sound information. They say the shipment might be imminent!'

'We've been down this path before and we keep drawing a blank. Did you pay for this news?'

'Of course. If they think their knowledge is of value they always have a price.'

'Which makes it worthwhile for them to invent something?'

Appleyard shrugged his shoulders angrily but said nothing.

'So what have you learned, Master?' Sam stepped in.

Tom recounted his meeting with Jonah. 'He's heard of suspicious activity near the Isle of Dogs. We must go there now to investigate.'

Sergeant Appleyard spoke up. 'Mr. Tallant, we are finally close to stopping a shipment from Southwark. If Skippon learns we missed it because we embarked on a fool's errand, and on the word of a Thames boatman of all people, it will not go well with us.'

Tom reflected on the sergeant's words. He had volunteered his services at Pym's request. Now he faced the threat of punishment if he failed. It was a sobering realisation, but overwhelmed by a growing anger. 'Sergeant, I completely trust the boatman in question and have reason to thank him for previous assistance he has provided.'

'They are renowned for gossip and tittle-tattle. Everyone knows you can't keep a secret on a wherry!'

'We do not have time to haggle.Your orders are to support me, but I cannot command you to comply with my decision. I am going with Sam to the Isle of Dogs. It is not sensible to divide our resources but, if you will not join us, I suggest you and Trooper White travel to Southwark and make your arrest. If you are right, I will make sure Skippon knows the gunpowder was captured solely on your initiative. But I can't waste another minute bandying words with you, Appleyard. Come Sam, sheath your bow and collect your arrows.'

Chapter 18

On the road to Banbury, Oxfordshire

Elizabeth stretched her back and groaned. The stage coach from London to Oxford had been uncomfortable, but her new transport to Banbury, a springless cart, was worse. She leant forward and tapped her servant on the shoulder. 'Edward, let us stop at the next inn and give the poor horse a rest.' Elizabeth sat back on her wooden bench. Edward had insisted she travelled behind him under the carriage's canvas cover, to escape prying eyes. She had spent the last three hours staring at his back. He was a giant of a man, his muscled frame filling his jacket, and she had to admit it was a reassuring sight.

Harvey's invitation had been sent from Worcester. In it, he mentioned the King would be marching to Shrewsbury to recruit desperately needed men. Elizabeth had set out for Oxford, hoping for further news there on His Majesty's progress. But, to her surprise, the town was quiet. Sir John Byron, commander of the Royalist garrison, had left with his troops to rendezvous with the King.

Elizabeth decided to remain in Oxford to rest and await further news. The situation was both fluid and confused. Reports were arriving in fits and starts, and it was difficult to sift the truth from the mass of rumours. To the best of her knowledge, the King had now left Shrewsbury, presumably returning to Worcester, and the Parliamentary force under the Earl of Essex was near Northampton, over eighty miles from the King. After three days without further information, she was chafing to renew her search. She must find Harvey before hostilities broke out. So she had chosen Banbury, as a rough midpoint between Worcester and Northampton, as her next destination.

The cart crested the brow of a small hill and the road ahead led to a large village. A number of manor houses surrounded a clutch of smaller buildings and at its centre, stood a church without its spire. They stopped at a tavern and Elizabeth began to leave her seat.

'Please stay here Miss Elizabeth, until I've checked it's safe to enter.'

Elizabeth sighed. 'It's a quiet village, Edward, please don't be tiresome. I have urgent need of a privy.'

Edward blushed. 'One moment my lady...' and ran into the tavern, returning a minute later. 'All seems clear, Miss Elizabeth' and helped her down from the cart.

'Please order some food and drink and find out where we are' Elizabeth instructed before striding inside. Edward trailed in her wake, shaking his head. Ten minutes later they were sitting by an open wood fire, crackling and spitting as new logs took light.

'Miss Elizabeth. I should not be eating with you. It is not proper.'

She looked around the empty parlour. 'Nonsense. We have the place to ourselves. And what if the landlord is the village gossip? We will have left within the hour.' She tasted her pottage. It was simple but wholesome and the mutton was fresh. The inn was clean and well maintained. The tavern keeper brought two mugs of beer to their table.

'Here we are my lady, a fresh brew from the barrel.'

'Thank you. This pottage is very good.' The man beamed and bowed his head slightly. 'What is the name of this village?'

'You are in Deddington, my lady, and this is the Crown Inn.'

Elizabeth took a sip of her beer. It had a clean, floral taste. 'Mmm, this is good also. Very refreshing. Tell me, are we near Banbury?'

'About six miles north of here. You take the Adderbury road.'

'And have any soldiers been here?'

The tavern-keeper's face darkened. 'Yes, they have, more's the pity. Treated us poorly they have.'

'What do you mean?'

'Have you seen our church?'

'With the collapsed spire?'

'Yes, it came down in a storm some seven years ago. We've been slowly building a new tower but the King's soldiers stole our bells last week, to be melted down to make cannon. Loaded them on carts and left. Some of us tried to stop them but were clubbed for our troubles. Now, even if we rebuild the tower, we'll have a church with no bells, and no way to call folk to worship. It's not right.'

'I'm sorry to hear that,' Elizabeth replied.

The landlord moved a little closer, twisting a cloth in his hands. Edward stood up, ready to defend Elizabeth. She put a restraining hand on his arm. 'It's all right Edward,' she said quietly and turned back to the tavern keeper. 'Please join us. What is your name?'

'John Birch, my lady, and thank you, I will. Forgive my presumption, but I don't think you're from these parts? You're from further afield, Oxford perhaps?'

'No, I have travelled from London.'

Birch's face brightened. 'So you must have news, about this turmoil? It's the Catholics, isn't it? Did those papists chase the King out of London? We're told to take sides, but against what? No Catholics around here. Up at Adderbury, the vicar and the village are at each other's throats, coming to blows. But how will that change anything…and what's to change? Now soldiers arrive. Something big is up, north of Banbury, there's talk of little else in the village…'

Realising his voice was raised, Birch paused. 'Begging your pardon, Miss. It's just that why must Englishmen fight and kill each other, sometimes from the same family? For what? It's unnatural. Ma says it's God's punishment for all our sins but I hope not. I pray to God everyday to end this madness that has descended on us all. He's the only one who can. I only hope He's listening.'

An hour later, they were back on the road to Banbury. Adamant she could not endure another minute in the cart, Elizabeth persuaded the landlord to keep it, in exchange for a second horse. She was not convinced the old mare was able to travel faster than a steady walk, but that would suffice as the roads were filling with groups of marching men. Encouraging signs of an army nearby, but which one?

The track ahead resembled a pathway recently travelled by heavy-footed giants. The surrounding vegetation on either side was crushed and churned into a broad stretch of thick, rutted mud, running like a vivid scar up the hill ahead. For much of her journey north she had wondered how she would locate William Harvey and the King's army. As she neared her goal, it became clear it would leave a pretty clear trail in its wake.

It had rained on and off for most of the last three days and the ground was saturated. Soon, it would be impassible. Ahead, a troop of infantrymen was labouring up the slope, weighed down by their muskets, bandoliers and armour. Some were holding fifteen foot ashwood pikes, deadly in close quarter battle but a burden to carry with treacherous ground underfoot. As she approached, she heard the soldiers grumbling in a language she did not recognise. On her travels. she had encountered broad accents, from Yorkshire to Somerset, but this was different. She and

Edward worked their way past the soldiers who barely looked up as they overtook them. She approached an officer at the head of the ragged column. 'Excuse me, sir. Do you speak English?' The man turned and stopped, surprised to be confronted by a woman on horseback in the middle of this field.

'As well as you, madam' and he touched the corner of his sodden hat in salute.

'But…'

'What are my men speaking? Why Welsh, of course, their mother tongue.' His exhausted horse was happy to stop. The officer patted its neck and gently urged it forward. The horse reluctantly renewed plodding through the mud, with Elizabeth riding alongside.

'I am pleased to present Sir Edward Stradling's troop of infantry, marching from South Wales to answer the King's call.'

'From South Wales? Your men have carried their pikes such a distance?'

'No, those are usually stored in the baggage cart, but they make it too heavy in such mud, particularly on this slope. So the pikemen have to carry them and manage the best they can. We have been accompanied by this infernal rain most of the way. I am hoping we are nearing journey's end.'

'I am also a stranger to these parts, but I heard the King's army is north of here, and when I saw the tracks, I decided to follow them.

The officer gave a weary laugh. 'I would caution against taking your lead from the military, madam. I wouldn't say this to my men but we are simply following the regiment ahead and I doubt they know where they are heading. You would think it hard to lose an army of many thousands, but I am not convinced our commanders know with any certainty where the enemy, or many of our own forces, are currently situated. My soldiers are tired and hungry and it does morale no good when they realise they are marching past a village they came through two days earlier.'

'You are walking in circles?'

'I fear so. This is the soldier's lot. But why, may I ask, are you here?

'I need to contact a gentleman in the King's retinue.'

The officer looked at Elizabeth and smiled. 'A sweetheart perhaps? Madam, your courage and devotion do you great credit, but this is no place for a lady.'

Elizabeth sighed but said nothing. It was the common assumption among the men she met on her journey. It was easier to leave it that way.

'Well, I would advise you keep your hood up, even if by some miracle we are eventually blessed with dry weather. Soldiers on the march feel entitled to whatever the passing countryside has to offer, and that means not only food and water, if you understand my meaning. I wish you a safe journey, and ask you to pray for our souls, for we know not what awaits us.'

At that, the officer tipped his hat again and pulled his horse around to walk down the column of soldiers trudging through the mire. He shouted a stream of Welsh at the troops who stiffened their backs and started to sing.

Chapter 19

On the Thames

'Lean over the side. You'll not foul my barky!'

Sam Barnes groaned, turned towards the river and emptied his breakfast into the Thames. Tom put a consoling arm on his shoulder but Jonah was not so sympathetic.

'Wretched landlubber,' Jonah murmured as he pulled hard against the swell. He was hugging the northern shoreline to avoid the worst of the choppy waters whipped up by the wind coming off the estuary. Tom knew Jonah was among the best boatmen on the river and watched his smooth, powerful strokes admiringly. They were making steady progress although even Jonah was finding it hard going.

They had met Dibdin at the warehouse and set off at pace downriver, passing the Customs House and the Tower within minutes. Jonah settled into a steady rhythm and Wapping Stairs soon appeared on their left. Sitting in the stern with Sam, he faced Dibdin and watched his face, a study in concentration as he powered though the water, his oars biting into the river's surface, pushing the wherry forward. The Thames bent to the left and they approached Execution Dock.

'No one on show?' It was the first words Jonah had uttered since they had left the warehouse. Tom noticed he had eased his stroke rate. 'How disappointing for you.' Tom grimaced at Jonah's jibe. The dock got its name from the practice of hanging pirates and mutineers on the wharf and leaving them to be submerged by three successive tides. He had heard a short rope was used for the hanging, meaning some victims would be choking, but not dead, as the waters edged up over their face.

'Nice area, this,' Jonah grinned wolfishly. 'Coming up on our left next will be Ratcliffe…a sailor's den if ever there was. You can enjoy every pleasure known to man down Narrow Street, and get your throat cut if you're not careful.'

Tom studied the shoreline and remembered Jonah's words about how little he really knew the river. He noticed a small shipyard on their left and the beginnings of a three masted vessel, the wharf lined with ship's chandlers. He had never seen it before. Was this their destination? But Dibdin kept on rowing.

Sam was clearly struggling, his face ashen white as he gripped the wherry's edge. He was from farming stock and always happier on dry land. The river started swinging in a deep turn southwards. 'Ratcliffe's in the lee of the wind, so I've slowed my stroke, ready for another dart down the Isle of Dogs…and before you ask, it's called that from Old Coppernose keeping his hunting dogs there.' Tom smiled at the name. By the end of his reign, Henry VIII was putting so much copper into coins bearing his image that, once in use, the thin coating of silver would soon wear off, starting at his nose. Strange how the name had stuck.

They reached the bottom of the Isle of Dogs peninsula and as they rounded the bend to head north again, were pushed back by the strong breeze. Jonah rowed closer to the shoreline and raised his stroke rate. As the prow bit into the choppy water, the boat started to pitch up and down and Sam's face turned green. The wherry battled its way north, the wind whipping cold spray into Tom's face. Few boatmen came so far downriver but Tom knew Dibdin's most profitable route was taking merchants to nearby Rotherhithe on the south bank, to inspect their ships under construction.

At last they reached the top of the peninsula and calmer water ahead. Jonah gently pulled towards the shoreline and an approaching jetty. The wherry bumped against a wooden post, which Jonah gripped tight. His breathing eased as all three recovered from their journey, warming themselves in the unseasonable sunshine, in the shelter from the shoreline, as the colour returned to Sam's face.

Jonah broke the silence. 'Right, journey's end for me. If you walk along the shoreline you'll soon come to a small estuary on the left called Bow Creek. This is the mouth of the River Lea, where it flows into the Thames. If you find a small sailing ship anchored at the mouth of Bow Creek, you'll know my information was correct.'

'This will be our gunpowder ship? So it's not hiding on a quiet wharf after all?'

'No, they'll be loading it the slow way, by row boat from the shore, one barrel at a time. It makes for a quicker escape if they need, and possible to do without drawing attention to themselves, if they've found somewhere quiet like this.'

Tom looked at the surrounding land. He couldn't see or hear a soul, except a group of dunlin squabbling on the shoreline. He thought of the busy docksides he had been searching and knew at once Jonah had been right. 'But how do they transport the barrels to such a remote spot?'

'Probably overland to the river Lea, then downstream to Bow Creek. No one would expect any roads worth the name in a place like this, but there's been a crossing point on the Lea for as long as I can remember. Started as a ford but became a bridge. So the path to it is a good one. '

'You think they're bringing the gunpowder from somewhere in London, down this route and stopping at the bridge?'

'Where they transfer it to the river, into the creek and onto the ship. Smooth as silk.'

Back on dry land, Sam was making a rapid recovery. Tom thanked Jonah and, a few minutes later, they set off on foot along the shoreline, crouching as they walked. They halted every fifty yards to peer over the surrounding brush and, as they rounded a corner, Tom signaled Sam urgently to get down. They shuffled forward on hands and knees to the brow of a small rise and peered into the mouth of Bow Creek, and a ketch anchored near the shoreline.

'There she is master, Jonah was right!' Sam whispered excitedly.

'Well Sam. It's *a* ship. Let's take a closer look' and he unstrapped the knapsack he'd been carrying since they left the warehouse, extracting a long, thin leather case.

'I was pondering on what was in your bag, master' Sam smiled. 'I thought it never left the warehouse, except when you were at sea.'

Tom opened the case and carefully withdrew a spyglass, over a foot in length. It was a Lippershey, a gift from his Uncle Jonas in Amsterdam. Tom only knew of four others in London. 'That's right Sam. My spyglass is precious and delicate, but I thought we would need it today.' He cleaned both the lenses with a soft cloth from the case before settling down, lying on the brush, to view the ship at anchor. The sky was cloudless and the air clear, the best possible conditions.

Tom was silent while he surveyed the ship and the shoreline nearby. There was little movement on board and no sign of a rowing boat. If this was their vessel, they had arrived in time.

The silence was broken by a shout from the shore. Tom scanned the bank and saw a figure running down a path towards the creek, waving his arms. He swiveled the spyglass to the vessel and saw two men appear on deck and run to the ship's side. After a shouted exchange, the man on shore disappeared behind a fold in the headland.

'I can't make out what they're saying master. What's going on?'

Tom studied the ship for another minute, long enough to recognise the unmistakable signs they were preparing to haul anchor and set sail. 'Quick Sam. I don't know how they've spotted us, but they're preparing to leave, and in a hurry. We must get down there.'

Sam pulled his sleeve. 'Look master, on the shoreline.'

Tom swivelled the spyglass to his left and his blood started to pump. A wherry had appeared from behind a bank of grass, its prow unnaturally high in the water. The boat moved forward revealing two men feverishly working the oars, and three wooden kegs sitting in the stern seat.

'Thank you Jonah. You never fail me,' Tom murmured as he carefully returned his spyglass in its case into the knapsack. He heard a cry from the wherry. The two rowers were making heavy weather of leaving shore and one had now missed his stroke completely and fallen inside the boat.

'Come on Sam. We can still catch them! No need to hide now.' Picking up his sack, he started sprinting towards Bow Creek. He stumbled on a hummock and gasped. His throat tightened at the thought of falling and breaking his spyglass. He would never be able to face his uncle again. Tom carefully watched his step as he ran down the slope to the mouth of the creek. The ground became level, a firm mix of small shingle and coarse sand. The rowers had recovered and were making headway towards the ship, encouraged by the men on board shouting and pointing at Tom and Sam.

They ran another fifty yards, the sound of Sam's feet crunching through the shingle behind him. But they were too late. The wherry was now in deep water and out of reach. He stopped and lent forward, hands on knees, gulping in air. The sun continued to shine, and he wiped his face with his sleeve. Sam slid to a halt behind him, his bow still strapped to his back.

'Let me swim out to them, master. I can tip the boat over,' Sam gasped and he started to unbuckle his quiver of arrows.

'No, Sam. I doubt you'd catch them now and they could beat you off with their oars anyway. Damnation! So close.' Tom stared at the wherry, the sun glinting on the ripple of water in its wake. Now the pursuit was over, it was almost a peaceful scene…reminding him of his trips on the river with Elizabeth.

Elizabeth…the sun…on the river…

He grabbed Sam's arm. 'Take some deep breaths, Sam. Calm your breathing.'

'Why master?'

'Because you tell me it helps you to shoot straight. What's in your quiver?'

Sam rummaged among the contents. 'It's my full kit, master. Bodkins , broadheads…ready for practice at the butts.'

Tom looked at him pleadingly. 'Please tell me you have some fire arrows in your sack?'

A dawning realisation came into Sam's eyes. 'I do! The archers were telling me how to fire a burning arrow. They were to show me after practice, in a quiet corner of the field, so I made up three or four last night.' The fire arrows were wrapped together in cloth. Sam started to unpack them excitedly, when he stopped and his shoulders sagged. 'But how can we fire them up Master, out here in the middle of nowhere?'

Tom was removing his spyglass from his sack. 'Prepare your bow, Sam, and leave the rest to me!

The wherry was nearing the ship. The men on board were pointing to the shore and jeering at Tom and Sam. 'Take your time, Sam. They've got to off-load those kegs yet. Choose your ground and get accustomed to the wind. It's dropped on the shoreline but remember the direction it was blowing on the journey here.' Sam stepped closer to the water and tested his footing in the sandy shale. Satisfied, he stretched his bow and threw strands of marram grass into the air to judge the breeze.

Tom was examining the lens of his spyglass and tentatively attempted to unscrew one end. It resisted slightly and then started to turn. 'Thank God for Dutch craftsmanship.' he murmured and removed the lens from the body of the spyglass.

'Now, Sam. Select one of your bolts and hold the end steady.' Sam held up the fire arrow. It had a long thin bodkin head, which was wrapped in cloth with a shiny brown coating, its needle-sharp point poking through the end.

Tom took a deep breath and held the lens up to the sun, above the arrowhead.

'Now steady, Sam' and he waited for the tell tale trail of smoke to begin.

Sam watched him intently. 'What exactly are we waiting for, master?'

Frowning, Tom stopped and gave the lens a polish before placing it again above the arrowhead. Still nothing. He glanced at the ship and saw the second keg being winched up the side. 'Come on. What's wrong with you?' he muttered as his anxiety grew. They must not lose the ship when they were this close.

Tom tried to picture Elizabeth. He'd seen her do this so often. He turned the lens over and gently tilted it from side to side. A white circle appeared on the arrowhead. He adjusted the angle of the lens and moved it closer until the circle narrowed to a pinpoint. In seconds, a thin trail of smoke appeared and the distinctive smell of pine.

Tom coughed. 'What's in it, Sam?'

'Black powder, additional saltpetre, vinegar and a little tar, wrapped in a cloth soaked in rosin.'

'Quite a brew!' Tom exclaimed as the smoke increased and, with it, a flickering flame. Sam held the arrow by its shaft and walked carefully to his firing position and carefully loaded the bow. He took a deep breath and, in one powerful movement, lifted the bow, bent his back and smoothly drew its string to his cheek. He stood perfectly still as the arrowhead crackled and burnt, before releasing the shaft into the blue sky.

A shout went up from the ship as they spotted the arrow arc through the air, leaving a trail of smoke, before dropping towards the sea. Tom held his breath. He knew it would be a miracle if Sam's first attempt found its target. Everyone stopped to watch the arrow's course. Tom's hopes were fading. It's going to overshoot. Only three left. But at the last moment it dropped and ripped into the topsail on the main mast. Tom watched the arrow hanging loose from the sail, embedded in the canvas. He waited, then saw a tell tale trail of smoke and flame rising from the mast. The sail was alight.

Tom slapped Sam on the back. 'Fine shooting, Sam! That will give them something to think about. With luck, the discharge from the black powder will spread the melting tar over the canvas. They won't put it out in a hurry.' Tom watched the first signs of panic on the ship's deck. The wherry was forgotten, the two men inside scrambling up the ship's side to join the others on deck. One of the crew was half way up the main mast.

Sam unleashed another burning arrow, reducing the angle of flight slightly, but this fell short, hitting the water with a loud hiss. Only two shafts remained. 'It's difficult to judge master, with the extra weight on the arrowhead, and the breeze is fitful.'

'I know Sam, but you've got to make these last two count! If they can put out the fire in the sail, they'll make their escape.' Meanwhile, in their rush to fight the fire, the two men had forgotten to tether the rowing boat to the ship's side and it was drifting towards the shoreline, with a keg of gunpowder on the stern seat.

Tom lit the third arrow and handed it to Sam. 'Should I aim for the wherry, master? It's an easier shot.' Tom weighed up the options. If they destroyed the wherry, it would trap the smugglers if the ship's sail became unusable. Fire was breaking out in the top rigging and two men were now aloft, hacking at the burning sail to set it free. Sam was eyeing the crackling tip of his arrow. 'Master, I must fire this shaft now before the heat burns through the rosin and ignites the black powder!'

Tom hesitated before shouting 'Shoot at the ship, Sam. The ship!'

Sam released the arrow but it spiraled to the left missing the ship by yards. Tom cursed. In his haste to get rid of the it, Sam had snatched at the shot. It had been a complete waste. 'Sorry master. Once the tip is well alight, it doesn't fly true.'

'It's not your fault Sam. Blame my indecision.' Tom surveyed the scene. The men up the mast had succeeded in cutting away the burning canvas and were attempting to pull it from the mast and dump it in the sea. 'We have one shot left in our locker. Take all the time you need, Sam. Try and land it on the deck.'

A bellow rang out from the ship. Tom was watching the two men struggling with the sail. As he looked, a blazing rope gave way and the burning canvas dropped towards the deck. One man on the mast grabbed it and was hanging on for dear life. Flames licked up the sail towards the sailor.

He shouted again but then was forced to release the flaming canvas with a scream. Tom and Sam looked on, fascinated, as the sail, by now fully ablaze, fell to the deck and disappeared.

'Jesu. It's fallen into the hold,' Tom whispered. 'It must be open to store the final kegs from the wherry…'

As one, the crew threw themselves overboard into the creek, both from the mast and the deck. As they surfaced, they struck out for the shoreline but it was soon clear some were unable to swim.

'Sam, we need to…'

A blinding flash consumed the sky followed by a brutal punching force, knocking them off their feet, as a roaring crash enveloped them. Three massive shocks, yet it was over in seconds. Tom sat up groggily, his ears buzzing with a high-pitched whine. He peered at the creek through the smoke, as hundreds of burning shards of wood rained from the sky. Where the ship had been, there was only empty water and smoking debris. It had been blown to Kingdom Come.

Sam was lying on his back, not moving. Tom shook his shoulder and he stirred and raised his head. The air was filled by a chorus of screams from alarmed seagulls, the hiss of burning wood landing in the sea, and desperate cries for help from the crew in the creek. Tom pulled Sam up to a sitting position. 'I think our mission has been accomplished. That's one shipment of gunpowder which will not aid the Royalist cause!'

They both staggered to their feet as Jonah's wherry came in to view from behind the headland to their right. Tom watched the boatman row circumspectly towards where the ship had been. He inspected the area before moving towards the nearest crew member thrashing in the sea, shouting for help. Within ten minutes, Jonah had pulled four from the water and was carefully bringing his overflowing wherry to the shoreline, where Thomas and Sam waited.

‘Sit still, you lubber’, Jonah shouted as a crewman tried to stand up, ‘or I’ll take you mid-river and drop you back in'. The man looked terrified and shrunk back onto the crowded floor of the wherry. ‘Take a hold at the front there. Pull me up onto the shore.’ Tom and Sam grasped the prow as it approached and heaved the boat from the water. Jonah shipped his oars and nimbly stepped out of the prow and onto the sand.

‘Well, quite a show. Fawkes himself would have been proud of that. They’ll have heard it in Lambeth Palace – lifted the Archbishop out of his bed.’

‘You were right, Jonah.’

‘Course I was, but I didn’t expect you to near remove us from the face of God’s earth! What if I‘d been near the ship?’

‘But you weren’t, and it was our only way to stop the thieves escaping with the powder. But don’t worry, you’ll get a good fee for this trip.’

As ever, the mention of payment had a soothing effect on the wherryman and his attention turned to the bedraggled passengers cowering in his boat. ‘What shall I do with these fools? Bringing dangerous cargo onto the river! If I had my way, I’d have boarded at night, tied them to the mast and set their barky alight.’

Tom ignored Jonah’s outrage. ‘Let’s get them on dry land. I’ve got questions to ask.’ The four crewmen were in a sorry state and in no mood to offer resistance. They were transported to the shore where they sat in a huddle shaking with shock, coughing up river water. Tom needed to go in hard while the stuffing had been knocked out of them.

‘We don’t have long. Before you know it, this creek will be swarming with Parliamentary soldiers. So let’s get to the point. I know you support the King, and this consignment of gunpowder was destined for his army. I also know you were tipped off about our arrival, because the alarm was raised before any of you could have seen us. Who was it?' The men stared at him, silent and sullen, and ignored all attempts to get them to speak, despite the ordeal they had just endured.

This was no good. He had to find the gunpowder's source, otherwise the attempts at smuggling would continue and next time might succeed. 'Alright, have it your way. If you'd given me the information I required, I would have let you go.' Jonah raised an eyebrow at this. 'As it is, I will tie you up and leave you here for the Trained Bands to arrive. Jonah, fetch a rope from your wherry.' Jonah paused and, with the shadow of a smirk, loped towards his boat, returning with a length of strong cord.

'I can help.' The youngest-looking man spoke first. Tom suspected he'd been close to drowning when rescued, his will to resist broken. One of the others lunged at him. 'Shut your trap, you fool.' Sam pulled the man off and held him tight as Tom helped the boy to his feet and led him away. 'Say anything and you'll be watching your back the rest of your short life,' a man shouted as the boy walked away. Sam kicked him hard in the ribs and he fell silent, holding his side.

Tom sat on a hummock of grass with the boy. 'What's your name?'

'Jack, sir'

'Well, you strike me as a sensible lad, Jack. I understand you support the King, and that was no crime until these recent confused times. So I mean you no harm.'

'Oh no, sir. I do not support the King. And I do not support Parliament. A pox on them all, I say.'

Tom was taken aback. 'So why are you part of this this dangerous plot?'

'We're starving at home. Father lost his job when his master closed his work shop to join the Trained Bands. Mother looks after my brothers and sisters. So I have to put some bread on the table.' The boy, probably no more than thirteen, was pale and shaking.

'So who tipped you off?'

'I haven't a clue, sir. We were simply told, all of a sudden, to get a move on.'

Tom sighed with exasperation. They were running out of time. 'So you don't know who's been stealing the powder?'

'No, and I'm not sure it was stolen anyway.'

This was hopeless. Either the lad was a half-wit or he was deliberately wasting their time. The boy sensed Tom's exasperation. 'I'm sorry I cannot answer your questions, sir. I thought my knowledge might be of use but you are clearly seeking other information.'

Jonah appeared at his shoulder. 'Time to leave, sharpish. There's a party of men coming along the shoreline.'

Tom regarded the lad. This was his best chance of solving the mystery and it was slipping through his fingers. In desperation, he changed tack. 'Where was the ship taking the black powder?'

'Never told us.'

Jonah started to walk towards his wherry. 'I'm off, with or without you.'

In desperation, Tom grabbed the boy's coat and was raising his fist when Sam stepped forward.

'Master! May I try something different?' Tom let go and shrugged his shoulders.

A sound from the shore signified Jonah had reached his boat and was pushing it back into the water. Sam knelt down and squeezed Jack's arm gently. 'Well, so far we have a very good idea of what you don't know. But you said you can help us. How's that?'

The boy looked downcast. ‘I’m sorry sir, only I thought you might want to know where the powder is made?’

Chapter 20

On the road to Cropredy, Oxfordshire

Elizabeth and Edward reached Banbury to find the town in disarray, urgently preparing for a Royalist attack. The name on everyone's lips was Prince Rupert, the King's nephew. Despite his relative youth, Rupert had fought extensively in the European wars and had an appetite both for a fight and any plunder he found. His reputation went before him and now the people of Banbury were in a panic.

They stopped long enough to change horses and replenish their supplies before heading north, towards Cropredy. Elizabeth knew William Harvey must be close and for the first time there was uncertainty in her heart. Had his invitation been serious? What would he say when they met? She watched the now familiar figure of Edward, leaning forward to pat the neck of his mount, as they continued their journey ever further from London. What must he think? The young lady of the house suffering daily discomfort or worse, instead of sitting at home, being waited upon?

As she travelled the Cropredy road, she had an overwhelming sense of standing between two armies preparing to kill and maim each other. At any moment they would emerge and crush her from both sides. Elizabeth had not slept well since leaving London, haunted by her Cheapside attacker. Last night had been terrifying, waking in a cold sweat as the masked man staggered towards her, reaching out, his body punctured by arrow shafts. Was she going mad? Her impetuous curiosity had led her down strange paths before but this was different by a large measure.

She controlled the fear rising in her chest. No, she needed to be here, at this moment. To witness the forces tearing her homeland apart and to do something, anything, to lessen the pain and suffering of those involved, with the help of William Harvey.

'Make way, make way.' Elizabeth pulled her horse off the path as a group of officers rode past, heavily armed and lavishly dressed. Their arrival made Elizabeth's new horse rear up and, before she regained control, she was pitched from her saddle, landing with a cry in the ditch by the road. She lay on her back, confused and dazed, aware of a hubbub of noise around her. She slowly raised her head to see Edward dismount and grab the reins of her horse. Next moment, a face came into view, peering down at her inquisitively.

'Good heavens. I thought I heard the cry of a lady in distress.' Embarrassed by her prone and undignified position, Elizabeth tried to sit up. 'No, dear lady, do not move without assistance. You may aggravate any injury you have sustained. Allow me to help.' And as the man bent to lift her up, she noticed the distinctive smell of rose oil. Elizabeth stood gingerly and cautiously examined her arms and legs. No bones broken, thank God, but her right shoulder was sore and her cloak covered in mud.

'Allow me to introduce myself. I am Sir Ashley Warburton. And may I apologise on behalf of my fellow officers for forcing you off the road.' Elizabeth experienced a flush of physical attraction as she looked into Warburton's eyes. They were a soft grey, full of gentleness. She had never seen their like before.

'Pray, why is a lady travelling the road to Cropredy, in the midst of thousands of men with violence on their mind?'

'I am looking for the King.'

'Aren't we all, both friend and foe,' he replied with a laugh. 'But for what reason?'

'I have been invited by William Harvey, the King's personal physician, to attend him and assist in the treatment of soldiers, should any be wounded in combat.'

The smile faded from his face. 'Then you will be busy, madam, I have no doubt. But I am not sure it will be any place for a lady's finer sensibilities.'

Elizabeth bridled at the suggestion. 'I believe I am strong enough to withstand whatever I witness. I will be too busy tending to the wounded.'

Warbuton was silent, appraising her. He started to speak but stopped himself, shaking his head slightly. He surveyed the stream of men and carts lumbering past them in the thick mud. 'I must catch up with my fellow officers. If you wish to find the King's party, they are quartered in the village of Edgecote, further up this road. Soon you will come to a fork. Most of the troops will go left but you must take the right hand turn, which leads for Wardington. Edgecote is the village beyond.' He mounted his horse and reined her in. 'I thank you for your consideration of my fellow soldiers. We are not used to such succor. Yours is a rare quality, Miss…?

'Seymour…Elizabeth Seymour.'

'Yes, a rare quality that touches me deeply. I wish you safe passage.' Ashley Warburton bowed in the saddle, pointed his horse north and galloped up the lane.

It was late afternoon when Elizabeth and Edward rode into Edgecote. Once off the Cropredy road they had made better progress and thankfully it was still light as they entered the village. It was not difficult to find the King's battle headquarters at Edgecote House. A stream of men hurried in and out of the main entrance, which was heavily guarded. They dismounted and, leaving Edward with the horses, Elizabeth approached a soldier guarding the front door, who stepped forward to bar her way.

'Where do you think you're going?' he called out gruffly.

'I am seeking William Harvey, the King's personal physician. He has requested my presence.'

The soldier laughed. 'Really? I bet he has, the old goat. Doesn't look like he's got it in him.'

Elizabeth regarded her muddy cloak and disheveled hair. To be mistaken for a camp follower! Well, that was a first, and she laughed at what her father would say if he knew. She fished inside her deep cloak pocket and pulled out her letter of invitation from William Harvey. She thrust it into the guard's hand, hoping he could read. The man studied the document and his expression softened. 'So, let me get this right. You've travelled alone from London, to meet the King and his surgeon?'

Elizabeth tried to calm her mounting frustration. 'No, I have my servant with me and, as you can see, I am here at the invitation of William Harvey. I have no expectations of meeting the King.' Or desire for that matter. She was weary and her shoulder was now throbbing, but the prospect of finally nearing journey's end spurred her on.

'Stay here,' and he disappeared into the house. More waiting. Elizabeth wasn't sure she would be able to take much more. Finally, she saw a welcome figure appear in the house doorway. William Harvey.

He strode towards her, in the gathering gloom, calling out: 'Elizabeth! Elizabeth! Is it you?' She ran towards him and they embraced. They had never been on such familiar terms but the realisation of what she had achieved overwhelmed them both. 'My dear child, I didn't think…how did you get here?...are you alone?'

Elizabeth described her journey with Edward, who was standing nearby with the horses. Harvey told the guard to find food and drink for the servant and their mounts. 'He'll have to find a space in the barn tonight. Edgecote House is full to the rafters.' Elizabeth nodded, explained the situation to Edward, and thanked him for his faithful service during their trip. 'I hope you sleep well, Edward, for who knows what tomorrow will bring?'

Elizabeth and Harvey entered Edgecote House, a bustle of activity.

Soldiers and servants crisscrossed the hall floor, carrying maps, platters of food, tables, and chairs. A sense of urgency and purpose pulsated throughout the building. Harvey led Elizabeth through the crowd and up the main stairway. On the landing they followed a corridor and near its end Harvey opened a door on his right. She entered a small room lit by a lantern and sat carefully in the chair proffered by Harvey. Any movement of her right shoulder now caused burning pain.

'Are you hurt, Elizabeth?'

She explained her fall and briefly outlined the journey from London. When she finished, she paused. 'You think me mad, don't you.' She needed his reassurance that her quest, her hunger to help and learn, rather than being hare-brained, was entirely rational.

'Of course not, Elizabeth. That's why I am here! A king on the campaign trail offers a number of research opportunities which would never come my way in Whitehall, particularly the study of injuries. I hope to conduct a number of dissections as, regretfully, there will be bodies available. I will request a suitable place to perform my post mortem investigations. I hadn't realised the hurly-burly of military campaigns. Always on the move! But now we are here, hopefully for a prolonged stay. I've toured the property and have my eye on a small pantry room which will serve my purposes admirably.'

'You intend to conduct your research here?'

'Where better? In his day, the King's father invited me to join Royal Hunts to examine fallen deer, under my knife, where they lay. I learned a great deal and hope to do so again, but this time about the human body. A number of casualties are anticipated and I will ask the officers to bring me a selection of cadavers while they are fresh. I must make the most of my opportunity, as this fighting between Englishmen will not last.'

Listening to Harvey, doubt started to cloud her mind. Desperate to flee London, she had persuaded herself Harvey's was right. If fighting was inevitable, better to gain medical knowledge that would help others in the future. She set off, expecting an adventure that would be smaller, briefer and less chaotic. She would ride to the Kings army, meet Harvey and observe his administrations to several wounded soldiers. The idea seemed risible now. All that she had witnessed on her journey told her any forthcoming battle could be a bloody, frenzied conflagration between thousands of men which, like as not, would settle nothing. She thought again about the Peace Party. But it was too late for that. She'd made her choice.

'We will study the effects of gunpowder on the field of battle,' Harvey continued. 'Burns, musket ball injuries and the impact of cannon. This will particularly interest you, my dear, given your expertise in salves and lotions, hence my invitation. With your spirit and determination, I should never have doubted you would find me, but when we commenced our tour of England -Nottingham, Shrewsbury, Birmingham - I did start to wonder! I never imagined such an ordeal.

'But now you are here, life will be much more agreeable.'

Chapter 21

Bolt and Tunn Inn, Alsatia, London

He shuffled down the lane looking for the familiar tavern sign – a barrel pierced by a crossbow bolt. He looked left, right and behind him as he approached the alehouse. He was becoming used to the landmarks of Whitefriars, or Alsatia as it was called by the locals, but that didn't make him feel any easier.

It was a lawless area, literally. The rules and regulations of the Church had prevailed while the Carmelite monastery still stood. But when that shut down in Henry's time, the local criminals repelled all efforts to impose state law in its place. Soon, it became a safe haven for all those fleeing justice and, once that happened, any attempt to bring Alsatia to heel were futile.

For the fiftieth time, he felt the sharp bodkin in his pocket. He experienced simultaneous reassurance and fear. This was no normal hairpin. At its head was a large rectangular spinel ruby, set with a sparkling diamond on each of its four sides. Underneath, white enamel provided the base for a gold pin that extended almost five inches from the ruby.

It was part of his collection and he was thrilled to be walking through the most thief-ridden street in London with the gemstone. If only they knew! But the jewel was safe with him, and he was safe with it, and the symmetry of this relationship made him gasp with pleasure. The coolness of the ruby nestled in his palm as he closed his fingers and made a fist, leaving the end of the pin protruding between his fingers.

He enjoyed the precision required to use a gold pin as an effective weapon. A punch in the eye would suffice, but it had to be accurate, and he always valued meticulous work.

He reached the tavern and walked into the front parlour where a man serving behind the counter nodded to him. He crossed the room and knocked on a door to his left. He went in without waiting for a reply and entered a dark room stinking of stale ale and tobacco smoke. He hated this place but his visits were an unpleasant necessity. He had the knowledge but not the means to make use of it. If only he had the brute strength and physical courage to render these men surplus to his requirements, just as he had with others like those loathsome, self-serving creatures at the Goldsmith's Guild. He had proven he didn't need them. If only it was that easy with Billy Boy and his gang.

'Oh, it's you'. The young voice, harsh and confident rang out from the gloom. Billy was sitting under the only window in the room, so encrusted with dirt it barely provided any light. 'Got some more work for us?'

He reached again for his amulet, the ruby hair pin. Faced by the sullen stare of Billy Boy, it was now more a screaming danger than source of inner strength. He hated Billy all the more for that.

'Yes. One is a jeweller, the other a private house. The jeweller will mainly have uncut stones, just landed from Serendib. And I have it on good authority that the lady of the house has an insatiable appetite for diamonds that has almost ruined her husband. It will be a good haul, but...'.

'But what? Please can we be more gentle? Tip toe in and just ask for the keys? Brush the floors and polish the furniture while we're at it? Is that what you were going to say?'

He stilled his tongue. He didn't object to Billy's methods, or his violence. They were a means to his end. But the gang were careless and noisy, something he'd warned about previously. It was only a matter of time before they were caught, and he didn't trust Billy. The little shit would give him away in a second if he thought it would improve his chances with the law.

Billy left his chair and sidled up to him. 'Now listen. When it comes to thieving, I had the best teacher you could find, God bless him. So leave that side to me. You and me, we've got a good thing going here. You get your gems and gold, and we get good coin from you, I won't argue with that.'

Billy Boy was his name but he was now a young man, strong and hard as stone. The street thief gripped his coat and pulled him closer, so they were face to face. Now! Now would be the time for precision, one swift movement and Billy the Bully would be floored, a spinel ruby standing proud from his face where his right eye had been. But he was terrified of the risk, and hid his craven fear under a mask of reason. He needed Billy. It would be senseless to kill him.

'We can't sell the jewels, not at the price you give us, and it would be too risky. And you, you couldn't break into a village church, could you? So let's not spoil our perfect arrangement, eh?'

Billy pulled him closer. He smelt brandy on his breath. The robber was living the high life now, thanks to him. But it would be over in a minute if the young man decided so.

'If I thought you were looking for a different partner...well, you've seen what me and the boys are capable of, haven't you?' His voice was now a low, hoarse whisper, dripping with menace. He nodded. 'Good, well let's get down to business then, shall we?'

Chapter 22

The battlefield at Edge Hill, Warwickshire

Elizabeth pressed down on the trooper's shoulder with both hands. Her palms were slick with his blood, which continued to seep from his wound. He flinched but said nothing.

'Rags, Luke. I need more, over here.'

A white faced, tousle-haired boy appeared with a handful of linen pieces. 'There's not many more after these,' he mumbled and scurried away. Elizabeth made a wad, which she pushed into the soldier's wound before wrapping it tight. The man raised his other arm weakly in thanks. He was barely conscious, his grey face etched with pain.

Despite William's Harvey's expectations and plans, they had been moved from Edgecote the next day and posted to the field dressing station in King's Leys Barn. It stood at the rear of the Royalist lines in the shadow of Edge Hill, a long ridge looming across the skyline behind them. In front of the barn, both armies were spread out in formation across the field of the Red Horse, which spread towards the villages of Great and Little Kineton in the distance.

She had waited nervously for signs or sounds of battle for several hours and, when it came, the impact was swift and terrible. Thirty minutes after the first cannon shots, the barn was filling up and, within the hour, they were inundated, every inch of floor space occupied by wounded and dying men. In London, she had packed a small box with healing ointments and creams, honey and eggs for their albumen and as much tincture of opium as she could get her hands on, but her meager supply was already beginning to run out.

Elizabeth surveyed a hopeless scene, stepping back as her servant Edward carried the lifeless body of a young ensign in his arms out of the barn. He was among the first she had treated, stabbed in the chest by a cavalry sword. She had dressed his wound with honey and administered a measure of her precious opium. His cries of pain had subsided and, ashamed, she realised she had forgotten about him until now.

She picked her way over the carpet of suffering and followed Edward outside. My God, it was Dante's Nine Circles of Hell - the cries and shouts of desperate men, punctuated by booming cannon and the crackle of musket fire, in a fog of choking, gunpowder smoke. A breeze briefly cleared the air to reveal soldiers in the vale below, as far as she could see, some in serried ranks, supported by galloping cavalry; others entangled in a storm of crashing pikes and armour, cheers and screams. Above it all, carried on the wind, she could hear the strains of a psalm, chanted by a phalanx of oncoming Parliamentary soldiers.

Elizabeth followed Edward to a small field behind the barn. Rounding the corner, she caught her breath. Empty when she arrived, it was now filling with corpses. The young ensign, no older than fifteen, was lowered to the ground with care. Another would be taking his place in the barn and, as she turned back, something caught her eye and a spasm grasped her heart. The Welsh officer she had met on the road to Banbury was lying dead at her feet, the front of his coat and shirt soaked in blood.

His lifeless eyes looked straight through her and, for a moment, the constant sound of battle disappeared. She instinctively knelt and touched his cold, white face. Tears filled her eyes. She had barely known him but, as a fellow traveller, he had shown her consideration and concern for her safety. She had liked his sardonic humour, as he lamented the army's ability to get lost. Sadly he had reached his destination and demise.

A cannon ball whistling overhead brought her back to the present danger. Edward, standing next to her, didn't move. He was in a daze, overwhelmed by the enormity of it all, his face drained of colour. She felt guilty he was enduring this nightmare because of her, but there was no time for that now as the long line of wounded continued to grow. She glanced down the queue, quickly assessing each soldier's condition and likelihood of survival. She approached a young man, rocking where he stood, nursing the right side of his face. She reached for his arm but he pulled it away.

'It's all right. I need to examine your wound, to see if I can help.'

'He won't let anyone touch it. You'd think his face had been pushed in a kitchen fire, poor sod.' It was the man's neighbour, the next in the queue. 'His musket blew up when he fired it. Not the first time I've seen it happen. It's because the King gives us poxy foreign rubbish to fight with.'

She persisted with the injured man and gently drew his hand away, His right cheek and forehead were burned, a single livid wound embedded with black powder dust. Miraculously, he had not lost his eye and there was no sign of life-threatening injuries. This soldier would hopefully live, so was worth her attention. Two hours earlier, she would not have made such an instant judgment. The thought alarmed her, but only for a second. There would be enough time later to reflect on this terrible experience. 'Edward, take him in. Give him the ensign's place on the floor and let him have water. I will see him presently.'

Elizabeth strode back to the barn, leaving the disappointed cries of other wounded in her wake. There were simply too many. It was all too much. Inside, she tried to ignore the fetid air and weary, frightened moans of the injured as she sought out William Harvey, who was performing surgery in a small back room.

Harvey was leaning over a cavalry officer lying on a rough wooden table. His face was white and covered in sweat, the uniform on his left leg drenched with blood. 'Now, young fellow. I believe you have a musket ball lodged in your thigh.' Elizabeth noticed Harvey's voice, quiet and matter of fact. 'I can see where it has entered your leg, but I cannot find an exit wound. It does not appear to have damaged your thigh bone and you have plenty of flesh in this area – signs of good living, eh?'

Harvey chuckled and the officer smiled weakly. 'So there's plenty for me to get at, and it will be better for your recovery if we extract this errant piece of lead, so let us proceed. My friends here will provide you with a leather piece to bite on…no, I strongly suggest you do not refuse it. No time for gallant gestures. But first have a good draught of this brandy. From my own cellar!' A man propped the soldier up who drained the glass of brandy and bit on a thick strap. He immediately ground his teeth into the leather with a groan as Harvey picked up the brandy bottle and doused the soldier's wound. 'Now gentlemen, if you would be so kind as to secure this gentleman's legs and arms…'

Elizabeth left the room, marveling at Harvey's detached manner. It reminded her of his dissection demonstrations she had attended at the College of Physicians, on Amen Corner in the city. She had wondered if the scale and brutality of the day would overwhelm him. It was certainly nothing like his expectations of a quiet room in Edgecote House to continue his research on one or two selected bodies from the occasional skirmish. Thankfully, he had remained calm and measured, although she wished he would work a little faster. Dozens were waiting to go under his knife.

She returned to the main room to examine the soldier with burns as a tall officer walked through the front door and approached her. At a glance she took in his fine leather boots and polished amour and assumed he was a member of the nobility.

'Mistress, get me help, urgently.'

'Why, sir? You do not appear to be wounded.'

At the sound of Elizabeth's voice, the officer stepped back, startled. 'Madam, please forgive my manner. I did not expect a lady of breeding to be here.'

'Breeding or not, I've always found it helpful to request rather than demand assistance. So, what ails you sir?'

The officer opened his mouth to complain but thought better of it. 'Please come outside, quickly.'

'Look around you. I am surrounded by wounded men, all requiring my care. There is not another inch of space to accommodate more, so these are the ones who will get my meager attention. All I can….'

Elizabeth stopped. Tears were running down the officer's proud face. He bent his head. 'Please, I'm begging you. It's my younger brother…'

She relented and followed the man outside the barn. He walked ahead of her and turned left, away from the queue of wounded. 'Sir, where are you leading me? Is your brother not with the other wounded?'

The man did not reply and started to run towards a thicket of trees twenty yards away. Elizabeth paused. Was this a trap? She dismissed the thought and followed the officer as he disappeared into the thicket. She caught up and peered through a mix of shrubs and the remaining autumn leaves of small trees. She picked her way through the low branches and reached a small clearing. The officer was kneeling beside another man, sitting propped against a tree. Two soldiers stood nearby, looking Elizabeth up and down. She leaned over the injured man. 'Is this your brother?'

'Yes. He has been stabbed in the side, beneath his breastplate. Can you help him?' The officer's face was a picture of misery. His brother wasn't moving.

She put her ear to his mouth and detected shallow breathing. 'Can you remove his cloak and breastplate?' The officer seemed reluctant. 'I need to examine the wound and there is no time to spare. He has lost a lot of blood. What is the matter? Here, I'll do it.' She lifted the cloak and stood back in surprise. The man was wearing an orange sash. 'He's a Parliamentary soldier. What's he doing here?' Fears of a trap reared in her mind again and she stepped away from the group. 'Are you all for Parliament?'

'Dear lady, please do not alarm yourself. My men and I are loyal to the crown but this cursed war has divided my family. My father and I support King Charles but my young brother and our uncle have taken sides with Parliament. It has broken my mother and, if young Hugh was to die, I believe she would not survive the grief.' Tears again formed in his eyes and he knelt to hold his stricken brother's hand.

'Hugh and I swore we would look out for each other, should we ever share the same battlefield. I was stationed at the rear with the King's retinue when I was told he had been injured, run over in Prince Rupert's cavalry charge that carried all before it. By then, the area was clear so I took two men and found my brother, lying wounded on the ground.'

'This is why you've concealed him in this thicket?'

'Even if we removed his sash, he might be recognised from the battle. The risk was too great.'

'So you tricked me into leaving the maimed among the King's men to attend a rebel who, for all I know, might have caused some of these wounds himself?'

The officer's shoulders sagged. 'It is dishonorable, I know it. But I can't stand by and let him die. We grew up together, and he is my other half. But if you are not of a mind to help, one of my men will escort you back to the barn.'

Elizabeth sighed and knelt at Hugh's side. He had not stirred since her arrival and she feared the worst. But he was breathing, so she pulled his cloak off. 'Unbuckle his breastplate. Slowly now and support his head when you lift him.'

Relief filled the officer's face. 'You will help him?'

'Just do it. I need to look at this wound.'

The breastplate was removed and Hugh was rolled gently on his side. 'Hand me your knife,' she said and cut away the bloodstained clothing around the wound. She found the entry point and cleaned away the crusted blood. She picked up the breastplate, examining its edge closely. 'It's as I thought. Now the wound is clean, you can see the point of incision is not as wide as you might expect. There's also a mark on the edge of the breastplate next to the wound.'

'Meaning?'

'I suspect his attacker thrust a dagger at Hugh, not a sword, aiming for his body behind the breastplate, but instead they caught the plate's edge. I suspect the thrust's force deflected the knife into his side, but as a glancing blow. Like as not, it entered his body travelling sideways, so will not have harmed his vital organs. Not a deep cut, so the bleeding has stopped.'

'Thank the Lord,' he exclaimed. 'So he will live'?

Elizabeth said nothing. Young Hugh was showing all the signs of approaching death, but why? She re-examined him, feeling his arms, shoulder and neck. She slipped her hand behind his head and stopped. She slowly removed her hand to find her fingers covered in crimson gore. With a sinking heart, she rolled him onto his front. His thick, shoulder length black hair on the back of his head was matted with blood. She gently probed the back of his skull, and found an indentation following a perfect curve. She returned the injured soldier onto his back and held his wrist for a while, looking at his face. He was barely a man, probably not seen his twentieth year. Like his elder brother, he wore a fashionable moustache, but his was soft, like down. Her heart ached at such waste.

'I'm sorry there's nothing I can do. I'm confident your brother would have recovered from the wound in his side, as long it did not become infected. But he also has a broken skull. The blow to his side would have been enough to unhorse him when Rupert's cavalry was pouring through the Parliamentary ranks. Lying on the ground, he has then been caught by a horse's hoof. You can feel the imprint of the shoe in his skull. He might have been trampled deliberately but I suspect it was an accident – a glancing blow from a passing horse. The rider may not have noticed.

'I know about the workings of the heart from the surgeon who is with me in the barn. Hugh has a pulse in his wrist, which signifies his heart beating. It is getting weaker. Stay with him. I suspect he does not have long to live.'

No one spoke. The sound of battle continued in the distance but it was now another world. A breeze caught the tree tops in the thicket, releasing a large bronze leaf which fell soundlessly and settled at the officer's feet. He bent down and slipped it in his pocket. 'Thank you for your care. One of my men will escort you back to the other wounded.' His voice was flat, drained of all emotion. In a daze he turned his back on Elizabeth and took hold of his brother's hand.

She walked away from the copse. It was a tragic tableau, and her sadness grew into anger. A family destroyed, like many others that day, because of men's stupid certainties they were right, and no other view can be countenanced. She thought of a woman sitting anxiously at home, awaiting news of her two sons. Such pointless waste.

She hurried back to the barn. The queue of wounded soldiers was now a sea of people, standing or sitting around its front. She walked past them and entered, to be confronted by a flustered William Harvey.

'Elizabeth. Where have you been? We have company. Come with me.' And he guided her back out.

'But William, I must attend to the wounded…'

'Sadly there is nothing we can do for them that will not wait five minutes,' and he ushered her to a wood store at the side of the barn. They walked behind the store and two young faces turned to meet her. 'Your Majesties,' Harvey declared, executing a deep bow.

Elizabeth stood, dumfounded. It must be the Prince of Wales and his younger brother the Duke of York. What on earth were they doing here? Prince Charles was dressed as a boy soldier, with polished breastplate and cavalier's hat, his face impassive. He nodded at Harvey and gazed quizzically at Elizabeth, who belatedly bobbed a curtsey. His face was expressionless despite the sights and sounds of battle surrounding him, but his younger brother James was frowning and clung close to him, holding his arm. She estimated James was no older than nine or ten and sensed the young Duke's fear, but resisted the instinct to gather him up in her arms.

The King's sons had their own escorts and one of them looked up at the sound of William's voice. 'Ah, there you are Harvey, where the devil have you been?'

'Please accept my apologies, my Lord. I have to instruct my assistant Miss Seymour, if I am to leave my post.'

Leave his post? What was William talking about? She opened her mouth to complain but Harvey seized her arm. He turned to the officer, 'One moment my Lord', and marched her away from the group.

'Elizabeth. I must be brief. The battle is getting a little warm around the King's position so he has ordered his children to retire to a place of greater safety. They have been placed in my care, here at the barn, so I am to sit with them in a nearby hollow, out of harm's way.'

'But William, there are dozens of men awaiting surgery…'

'It cannot be helped. My duty is to the King. I must leave you to do the best you can.' Harvey's face was impassive. The detached manner of the surgeon remained. Elizabeth knew it was useless to speak further, so she walked past Harvey and approached the young Duke of York, kneeling in front of him, face to face. She looked into his eyes.

'Sire, I can see you are brave and not in need of any protector, other than his majesty your brother.' At this, the Prince of Wales nodded gravely and squeezed the young Duke's arm. But I recommend Mr. Harvey's company. He is a wise man who has taught me a great deal. He has much knowledge to share, and good stories to tell.' The young boy nodded, biting his lip, his eyes filling with tears. Elizabeth gave him a reassuring smile, stood up and walked away, without a word to Harvey or the others.

In the barn, a palpable shock had descended on the hundreds of waiting wounded. Whatever they had expected from the day, it was not this. She had tried to help and gained important knowledge, but was overwhelmed by the sheer scale of suffering. The sun was dropping lower in the clear sky and the temperature falling. Her medicine bag was empty. Nothing more could be done.

She wandered into Harvey's back room. The wooden table where he had operated on the soldiers was now empty, saturated in their sticky, drying blood, the floor littered with the heavily stained uniforms cut from his patients. She rummaged through the mess and found what she was looking for. In a daze, she lifted Harvey's brandy bottle to the fading light. A little remained. Elizabeth pressed the bottle to her lips and tipped it upwards. The fiery liquid burned her mouth and throat. Good, she could feel that. She could still feel something.

She dropped the empty bottle on the floor and walked back to the main room, staring at her patients. She doubted many would survive the night. Inside, she laughed bitterly at the memory of those who said the war would be over after one encounter. She always thought it a forlorn hope. Now, having witnessed the savagery in the shadow of Edge Hill, she knew it for what it really was - a bloody fool's dream.

Chapter 23

Hounslow Heath, west of London

Tom lay among a patch of scrub and steadied his arms. Lifting his spyglass to his eye, he scanned the buildings in front for signs of activity. It was early morning, not fully light, and the cold from the ground seeped through his clothes. He checked the heath for signs of frost. Autumn would soon turn to winter.

The buildings were spaced well apart and separated by tall earthworks. Were these designed to limit the damage, in case of an accidental explosion? Elizabeth would know, having made gunpowder herself and, not for the first time that day, he wished she were there, but this time for her expertise. She would be a welcome change to Sam whose constant worrying was starting to wear him down.

'So, you think we are safe here, master? T'is a place of great danger, a black powder mill.'

Tom understood Sam's nervousness, having witnessed the ship's utter destruction, but he hadn't banked on this level of fear.

'I heard of one mill round these parts blowing up without any warning. Poor beggars didn't stand a chance.'

'Not a bad way to go, surely Sam. Like a candle snuffed out.'

This silenced Sam but Tom sensed his bookkeeper was bristling with tension, not helpful for silently breaking into the mill. He was tiring of this wild goose chase and, having located the gunpowder's source, was tempted to hand the matter over to Philip Skippon. But what if their young informant was wrong? No, he had to confirm this was the source of the smuggled powder beyond any doubt, and then Skippon was welcome to it.

Time to take a closer look,' said Tom and, standing up, caught the horrified expression on Sam's face. 'Let's be doing this. We will take every care and when we have established the facts, I promise you will never see a powder mill again.'

Sam got to his feet reluctantly and they walked briskly across the heath, keeping low to the ground. In the early morning stillness they heard the water flowing in the nearby river. They reached the first earthwork and paused, listening for signs of activity, but all was quiet. They followed the wall of soil into the complex of buildings. It provided perfect cover and soon they were at the centre of the mill. Again they stopped and, hearing nothing, Tom decided to break cover. He walked into a clearing between two wooden structures and beckoned Sam to follow.

'I think we're the first here, Sam,' Tom whispered. 'Let's find out what's inside.'

He walked to the first building. It was heavily locked, as was the next. This made sense given what might be inside. Not the place for a blundering thief, searching by lantern light. He considered forcing one of the locks but the thought of one spark in the wrong place stilled his hand. Sam's fear was catching.

Tom stood in the clearing, considering what to do. A voice nearby hissed at him. 'Master Tallant. Over here.' He frowned at Sam who shrugged his shoulders.

'Over here. To your left.' Tom turned as Sergeant Appleyard stepped from behind a mound of barrels and hurried towards them, furtively glancing left and right.

'What on earth are you doing here, Henry?'

'I was about to ask you the same thing. Let's find cover,' and he led Tom and Sam inside a small wooden hut that he saw was open. He turned to Tom, his eyes alive with excitement. 'You were right, Master Tallant. Southwark was another dead end. But we found a fellow there who knew of a mill and would tell us where, if I met his price. I was loath to throw good money after bad, but was desperate for a breakthrough, and his information brought me to this location. Is it a good sign you are also here?'

'I believe so, Appleyard. My search was more productive. We discovered a ship loading up and setting sail at Bow Creek, near the Isle of Dogs. Two of us weren't enough to capture it, so Sam set it alight with fire arrows.'

'Of course, you had your bow with you for practice at the Finsbury butts!' the sergeant exclaimed and slapped Sam on the back.

'When they saw the ship was alight, they got off pretty sharpish.

'How were you able to fish them out of the creek?'

'Luckily, the boatman who had taken us downriver to the ship had waited. He brought them to the shore.'

'And they told you where the powder was made?'

'Yes. They were shaken by the experience. Their information led us here to Hounslow.'

Appleyard gripped Tom's arm and shook his hand vigorously. 'Such news! The powder is destroyed and we have stopped the supply! Skippon will be delighted.'

'We've stopped *this* shipment but unless we stop the source, there will be more, which is why Sam and I are here. Once we have established beyond doubt this is the source, I will put the matter in Skippon's hands.' A noise to their right stopped the conversation. They kept stock still, ears straining. There it was again.

A man's voice, humming softly to himself, followed by a rattle of chains and the groaning of a gate opening on rusty hinges.

'The first workers are arriving. What shall we do?'

'I have examined several buildings and all are locked.'

'Yes, they're well secured.'

Appleyard shook his head. 'Looks like we'll have to sit tight, in hiding, and wait until the workers open up, then find a way in, under cover, and see what we can discover.' It was a risky plan but Tom could not think of another way to gain entry. They hid behind a pile of empty barrels in the hut after pulling the door shut.

Sam stared balefully at the barrels. 'Are you sure they're empty, master?'

Appleyard smiled. 'You are right to be nervous, Sam, sitting in a gunpowder mill. But you will be safe if you take care. You're not partial to a pipe by any chance?' and he winked at Tom.

Tom thought about Elizabeth, her love of tobacco and her previous experiments with gunpowder, and shook his head.

'Where's Trooper White?'

The smile fell from Appleyard's face.

'Where, indeed? We were wasting our time in Southwark when he disappeared. Slipped away one night from our lodgings.'

'We know the crew loading the ship at Bow Creek was warned of our arrival,' Tom said. 'We can't be sure whether they had spotted our approach but…'

'Damn him! On our way to Southwark I told him where you were looking for the powder. I said you were wasting your time and he agreed. He had family in Southwark and that night I gave him permission to meet them for a drink or two. His bed was empty the next morning and I thought he was nursing a bad head. When he never returned, I had him marked down as a deserter.' At this Appleyard spat on the floor.

Tom was surprised. 'Deserters? Is that a problem?'

'Oh yes, We have too many. Join the Trained Bands in the first flush of excitement, before sloping off at the prospect of some serious fighting, especially if their mothers get working on them, putting doubt in their heads. But White's worse than a deserter. That whoreson is a traitor to the King! I've heard since that he's gone over to the other side, trying to sell what he knows to the highest bidder. I've half expected to see him here, tipping off the owners!'

'So, you carried on the search alone and came up here?'

'What else could I do? Can't let those bastards get their hands on powder, to blow our boys to pieces. And I certainly won't let a treacherous runt like White get the better of me.'

Tom studied Appleyard's face, flushed with indignation and anger. The noise outside increased. 'That must be the waterwheel on the river, starting up. The day's production is underway. Time to take a look.' Appleyard got up and pushed the hut door ajar. Tom glanced at Sam who seemed troubled.

'Wait a moment.' It was Sam, who had stood up with the sergeant. 'Will it not be more dangerous for us to venture out now the workers are all here.'

Appleyard turned. 'No. The workers will be inside preparing the different ingredients. It is hazardous work and they keep all doors shut.' He moved again to step out but Sam shook his head vigorously.

Tom's patience with Sam's timidity was exhausted. 'Come Sam, have some courage. You cannot hide in here. It will be safe enough outside and we must get proof of what is happening.

Sam leapt forward and threw himself at Appleyard, clapping one hand over the soldier's mouth. They both landed with a crash on the floor at the entrance to the shed.

'What the…'

'Quick master, help me secure him. There's something wrong about our sergeant. If I am incorrect I will take any punishment coming but I think our lives will be in peril if you let him walk through that door!'

Appleyard was spread-eagled on the floor struggling to throw Sam off. 'You'd better be right. Lift him up but cover his mouth.' Appleyard was writhing and thrashing about, his cries muffled by Sam's large hand. They sat him upright but he continued to kick out with his legs.

'Be quiet, you'll have us discovered…' Tom hissed. 'No, that's what you want, isn't it? Sam, I think you're right. Appleyard, desist immediately or I will have to shut you up.' The soldier's eyes were wild with anger and the veins on his neck bulged. He started to thrash around again. Tom sighed, stepped back and hit him hard on the jaw. His head slumped and Sam stepped away.

'And there'll be more of that if you make any more noise.'

Tom peeped through the gap in the doors. Good. No sight or sound of anyone approaching, only the thunk-thunk-thunk of the waterwheel fully up to spe

He returned to Sam. 'Quickly, tell me your concerns.'

'He knew too much about Bow Creek. Let slip a few things that he could only know if he'd been there. He asked how we rescued the men from the water, but you had not said the ship was anchored off shore. For all he knew it was being loaded from the quayside. I thought maybe he'd made an assumption. But when he congratulated us for destroying the powder, I became convinced something was wrong. Your story was interrupted because of a noise outside and we began talking about Trooper White. He was more eager to tell us about his desertion than ask the obvious question.'

'What had happened to the powder on the burning ship.'

'Exactly. Because he knew it had been blown up.'

'He was there, at the creek?'

'He must have been and then set off by horse, straight back to Hounslow Heath to alert his fellow conspirators.'

Appleyard was slumped on the floor, his eyes now open.

'Is this so, Sergeant?'

Appleyard sighed and shifted his position. 'It's true enough. When I think of the time we took loading so much powder on board that accursed ship. One more day, just one more day, and we would have been away! But it's gone now, thanks to your infernal arrows,' and he kicked out at Sam.

Tom punched him again and Appleyard cried out. Sam again covered his mouth. 'Master, we must keep him quiet!'

Appleyard's eyes were wild with anger and pain, but he quietened again. Sam slowly released his hand from his mouth. Appleyard spat again on the floor and turned on Tom, whispering hoarsely. 'If I wasn't held down, you would not be so free with your fists

'There'll be more if you don't tell us what we need to know.'

Appleyard grinned. 'It matters not. You will never escape alive. When you blew up the barky I rode here to warn the others. I knew you would get the truth out of one of those on the ship.'

'But why this mill? There are dozens around London.'

'Not all include the King's friends among their workforce. A group of them have been skimming the odd keg from the regular production for months now. This is why it's taken so long to build up our stock on the ship.'

'So the owners are not for the King?'

'No. They want to keep their noses clean and make their profit. Pym asks for powder and they're happy to sell it, the dogs.'

Tom again heard voices nearby and signaled Sam to silence Appleyard. The voices became louder. Perhaps it was workers not part of Appleyard's plot? Was it worth the risk - leaving their hide and asking for their master, the mill owner?

Tom carefully peered through the crack in the door and to his relief saw the group of men approaching included Trooper White. 'It's all right. They're friends.'

Appleyard started to struggle again as Tom slowly opened the door and called to the approaching men. 'Trooper, it's Thomas Tallant. We've captured your errant sergeant.'

He stepped back as White entered. Appleyard pulled his mouth away from Sam's hand.

'Well done, White. Your timing is excellent. Tie these two up and be ready to leave in five minutes. We have an appointment with the King and his approaching army.'

Chapter 24

The Royal Exchange, Cornhill, London

Elizabeth shouldered her way past the crowd gathered at the entrance to the Royal Exchange. She left a trail of indignant merchants in her wake as she pushed through the throng to reach the centre of the trading floor. She searched the crowd. She was the only woman in the room, as far as she could see, and was attracting stares and disapproving looks. Then she spotted her quarry.

'Mr. Cooke, Mr. Cooke. I must speak with you at once.'

The jeweller was deep in conversation with two other men who looked up at Elizabeth, startled by the interruption.

'Ah, Miss Seymour. I didn't see you there. Please allow me to…'

'I must speak with you now, somewhere private.'

Cooke gestured to the other men. 'I just need a minute to finish my conversation with…'

'No time for that. We need somewhere private now.'

Cooke paused, looking bemused. His two companions were scowling at Elizabeth. One stepped forward and inspected her with disdain. 'Did you invite this…woman into the Exchange, Robert?'

'Err, not as such…, excuse me gentleman. This behaviour is most unusual. I can only assume something is badly awry,' and he took Elizabeth by the arm and walked her to a corner of the Exchange. She noticed he was limping and lagging behind, as they climbed a flight of stairs to find an empty office. Cooke closed the door behind them, a pained expression on his face. 'My apologies for trailing in your wake, Miss Seymour. I am frequently burdened with gout.'

He stood in front of her, red-faced and flustered. He patted his brow with a handkerchief. She was momentarily lost for words. Her mind was spinning and her head started to ache. The room was swaying and she sat on a nearby chair to steady herself. Her daily liquid tribute to the much mourned Galileo was catching up with her.

'Miss Seymour. Are you all right? You look quite flushed.'

'Of course I'm not all right. Would you be if you were taken by a snarling young wolf in a dark alley and threatened with death! He'd been following me, Cooke, he knew about our investigation, he knew about me, he knew about YOU!

How that can be? He gripped my arm and shook me like a wet dog. He made it clear. If I was to take this business any further, he would stop me, and for good. And he was deadly serious.'

Cooke looked aghast, twisting his handkerchief in tight knots in his hands. A thought grew in her head. Even though his name was mentioned by her attacker, perhaps Cooke didn't know what had happened?'

'But when was this outrage, Miss Seymour? I have not seen you for several weeks.'

'That's because I left London immediately. I was terrified.'

'Oh, thank goodness. He will believe you have heeded his warning, as indeed you must, now you have returned. I didn't think anything more would shock me in this tortured time, but this…' and his expression distorted by anguish. 'It's a complete breakdown in all that I love about my country. God has forsaken England and all we once stood for…decency, respect for order, love of our fellow man. For you to be assaulted and threatened by a total stranger is barbarous…' and he paused to wipe away his tears.

Elizabeth looked at Robert Cooke's face, now drained of colour. Either he was telling the truth and knew nothing about her attack, or Cooke was missing his vocation treading the boards of the Globe. No, she was satisfied that whoever was responsible for her encounter with the petrifying man in the mask, it was not Robert Cooke.

The thought calmed her, as did the distance it meant must still exist between her and her assailant. She was no closer to finding him, but did she want to? The initial shock of her encounter had dissipated now time had passed, and once again she was beginning to feel stirrings of resentment. Without her wishing it, her spirit was blowing on these embers, until a flame of determination was rekindled. Yes, she would continue the chase and to hell with the masked man.

There had been a pause in the conversation, while Cooke regained his equilibrium. Now he coughed and decided to turn the conversation to a more pleasant topic. 'At least you were able to leave this madhouse we call London for a few weeks of rest and recuperation, in the country perhaps?'

Elizabeth shook her head disbelievingly as her memory was dragged back to the senseless slaughter in the shadow of the Edge Hill. She reached into her pocket for her pipe. She wanted a smoke, but more than that. She desperately needed a drink.

Chapter 25

The village of Colnbrook, west of London

The cart lurched as its wheels found yet another hole in the road. Tom winced as the rope binding his wrists dug into his bruised flesh. Sam lay next to him in sullen silence. Like Tom, he was gagged and his hands tied behind his back.

As he gazed through a gap in the roof canvas, he saw the light was fading. The day was near its end and it was getting colder by the minute. He'd lost any sense of how far they had travelled and in which direction, but he was hoping for a better idea when the stars emerged. Throughout the journey, all he heard was the cart's creaking and the oaths of the driver, cajoling his old horse to keep moving. Occasionally he noticed the drumming of hooves as riders galloped past and the tramping feet of men on the march, mixed with shouted commands and the sound of women cursing and shrieking with laughter. Finally, he suspected journey's end was near as the cart began to stop and start. Sure enough, the next halt was much longer as a desultory argument broke out between the driver and a guard, standing to one side of the cart. Both sounded tired and disinterested.

'So, where do I put these two?'

'You tell me. It's Bedlam here. And you won't find a room anywhere. All taken by the officers for their overnight billets.'

'I'm told they're needed for questioning. Could have useful information. Not worth my life to lose them.'

'Find a quiet corner in this field, tie them to a tree for the night and keep guard. There's no officers to take them now.'

The driver cursed and the cart pitched to one side as the man hauled himself back on board. They started again and minutes later came to a final halt. By now it was close to dark. The canvas was flung open and a burly figure leaned forward and, grasping Sam's arm, pulled him out. He landed with a groan on the grass below and was dragged by his hair to a nearby hedge.

'Sit still there, you. Don't move or your mate's dead.' The man returned for Tom and manhandled him next to Sam. The driver picked up a length of corded rope and tied them together, sitting back to back, before securing the line around the trunk of a sturdy hawthorn in the hedge. He climbed into the back of the cart that was facing them and, within minutes, the night air was filled by the sound of steady snoring.

In this new position, Tom twisted his body to test the ropes binding the two of them. They were still secure and, despite his best efforts, he'd been unable to stretch the cloth gagging his mouth, which was till clamped tight, making speech difficult. He attempted to check on Sam but abandoned any conversation when all he elicited were a few grunts. Sam didn't appear to be in pain, but his spirit seemed broken. Tom could only conserve his own energy and pray the rain didn't start.

He needed to think and had the whole night to do it. He guessed they were heading towards the King's army. Looking at the sky, now lit by the emerging stars, he estimated they had been travelling broadly northeast. It was rumoured the King had marched his army to Oxford after the battle at Edge Hill, but if Tom and Sam were now close to Charles he must have changed his mind and returned to approach the capital. If the King was heading towards

London from the west, their paths would likely cross, but at what point? And where was the Earl of Essex and the Parliamentary army?

Tom did not understand the hesitancy on both sides. Surely London was the prize? Charles had been a fool to leave it, the centre of the nation's wealth but now he had an opportunity to make amends for his initial blunder and re-impose his control.

And what about Appleyard? He was furious with himself for believing Trooper White's defection. Why should it be true when the sergeant had lied about so much else? He cursed his naivety, inviting capture by calling the trooper over! Most of the millworkers were not part of the plot. If he had spoken to anyone else he might have been safe. But he had to choose White!

No doubt Appleyard had travelled ahead of them as they slowly made their way to the Royalist camp. He would be waiting for them in the morning, a meeting Tom was not looking forward to. In truth, he had very little information of value to the King, but that wouldn't stop Appleyard attempting to extract it with his fists.

It was not a comforting thought. He tried to clear his mind by looking again at the stars. Quite often, Elizabeth had picked out patterns for him such as the constellation Ursa Major but, without her help, Tom always struggled to find it again among the thousand pinpoints of light above him. His eyes became tired and soon his head drooped on to his chest.

The next day was worse than Tom had feared. Appleyard arrived in the morning and took them blindfolded to a stone barn, and found a quiet corner for his men to do their worst. He took pleasure in refusing to believe Tom had little information of use. He knew more than Tom about the gunpowder smuggling and the destruction of the ship was, by now, common knowledge. What more could he tell him? And soon Tom realised his mistreatment was really driven by Appleyard's fury that his gunpowder plans had been thwarted.

After one particularly brutal beating, Tom lost consciousness and that seemed to satisfy his tormentor, who didn't return. He came to in darkness and drifted in and out of painful sleep throughout the night.

Tom was woken hours later by a hand gently shaking his shoulder. Painfully he raised his head and peered at the figure bending over him. His swollen left eye was almost closed, and matted blood covering his right eye made it difficult to open. A soft handkerchief was being carefully applied to clean away the blood. Perhaps this was their method. Show him compassion, so the next beating would be harder to take.

'Animals! Damn, damn, damn them. My poor Thomas.'

Tom was startled by the familiarity of the voice.

'Barty? Is that you?' he croaked.

'I am ashamed to say it is, Tom and that I support the same cause as the brutes who have mistreated you so badly. Can you sit up a little?'

Tom tried but his body protested. His mind flashed back to the blur of punches and kicks raining down on him as he curled in ball, hoping in vain to protect himself. He tried again and, with Barty's help, shuffled into a sitting position. He groaned and felt his face.

'I fear I'm not good for much at the moment, Barty.' He tried to clear his head. The air was thick with the smell of horse muck and hay. He remembered the barn was a makeshift stable, but now it was empty. Had the King's army taken to the road again? 'Where is this place, Barty? Why are you here?' He suddenly looked around with a start. 'And where's Sam?'

'Your bookkeeper? I have not seen him but I will get a search party organised right away.' Tom was filled with a sense of dread. What had Appleyard done to Sam?

'Here, Tom. Take a little to recover your senses,' and Tom recognised Barty's ever-present flask of brandy. He swallowed a draught, appreciating the warmth. 'We are in the village of Colnbrook, to the west of London. I came here yesterday with a group of Parliamentarians to explore the possibility of peace talks with the King.'

'What? The King is here?'

'He was. We left last night, when the talks concluded, and the King retired to Windsor awaiting Parliament's further deliberations on our discussions.'

'So, we may have peace? The war is over?'

'Well, I dared to hope so until I returned to Colnbrook today and found the place deserted.'

'The army has travelled with the King, to Windsor?'

'Heading west? Away from London? Yes, it would be encouraging if it were true, but I'm told instead they have marched east towards Hounslow Heath where they intend to assemble.' Tom gave a hollow laugh. Appleyard had thrown him and Sam into the back of a cart and gone in search of his masters in the King's army. In the end, he could have saved himself the trouble. If he'd waited at the mill, the army would have come to him.

'If you think the King is planning an attack, Barty, you should know there is a ready supply of gunpowder on the Heath, from a number of mills situated there.'

'It's as I feared. I think his majesty has once again been ill advised and decided to mislead Parliament about his true intentions, so he can get closer to London and re-arm. This will completely undermine those who are working for peace, like myself.'

'But why did you come back to Colnbrook?'

'I heard a rumour that a Member of Parliament had been captured by royal forces and was getting rough treatment. I hoped to stop it, if it was true. I had no idea it was you. But why did your captors abandon you?'

'I think they finally accepted I had little information that would earn them coin or high praise from their commander, and when the order came to quickly break camp for Hounslow, they left me behind. But what have they done to Sam?'

'I'll arrange for the village to be searched. A small reward for his safe return should be enough. But what about you? You need to rest but getting back into the city from here will not be easy, and I'm not sure you are fit enough for the long ride west around London to reach your family in Clerkenwell.'

The last time Tom had seen Barty was before his decision to join Skippon in the Trained Bands. The troops blocking the King's way into London were now Tom's allies, not enemies, and he and Barty were on opposing sides, a ridiculous situation.

Not for the first time in their friendship, Barty moved quickly to ease any difficulty. 'I sense our positions have changed somewhat, since we last met?' Tom nodded. 'I assumed so, if you were roughed up by a Royalist soldier, although I am finding uncouth villains on both sides.'

'I have been offered an officer's position in the Trained…'

'I have no need to hear the details, Tom. I am sure, whatever your choice, it was driven by a good conscience and a wish to do the best for those around you. The less I know the better, in case anyone, in the future, attempts to extract information about *you* by fair or foul means. What does your father think?'

'That I am mad to get involved, with either side.'

'Keep your head down and concentrate on the business? Yes? Well, I think we're a little beyond that, don't you? So, the question now is how can we slip you past a Royal army to reach the relative safety of the Parliamentary defences of London? Well, let's find Sam and come up with a plan, shall we?'

Chapter 26

Cheapside

Elizabeth stood in the shadow of an overhanging gable roof, on the north side of Cheapside, rubbing her hands together. It was a bitter October afternoon and her spirits were flagging. Once again she leaned forward to survey Goldsmith's Row opposite before darting her head back.

Cheapside was quiet. The food sellers had decamped as usual at mid-day and the cold that had kept many other shoppers away penetrated her thin dress and shawl with ease. For the first time she appreciated what an ordeal winter must be for the poor of London. Her disguise was vital for her safety, but she was not certain it would be possible to endure the icy stabs of pain in her hands and feet much longer. She reached into her tie-on pocket and withdrew a bottle of arrack, a gift from Tom last Christmas. It had sat unused in her study ever since, but today it helped to repel the cold. She drank it straight from the bottle and paused, trying not to cough. It amazed her that the sap from a coconut flower made such a powerful liquor.

It was the second day she had been monitoring Goldsmith's Row in secret. Her hiding place was close to the scene of the attack by the masked stranger in the fog. It had been difficult to revisit this place and now the waves of terror were returning. Tom would be furious if he knew she was there, yet she longed for his reassuring presence and felt his absence more with each passing day.

In the days after her attack, her mind had gone over and over what had happened. How did he know her name? And why was his voice familiar? Also, the stranger must have been prepared for their confrontation, otherwise why would he have a mask?

She kept following this circle of questions to the point of exhaustion and she was forced to realise she had nothing to work with, except one small piece of information that might be beyond coincidence. There was little doubt her hooded assailant was responsible for the jewel thefts, otherwise why try to scare her off? And the attack happened near Goldsmith's Row. So perhaps the man had a link to someone there and, when he realised she was heading in that direction, decided to intervene to scare her off?

Initially she was excited by this thought but, on reflection, realised it was an obvious conclusion. The thieves needed inside information on where to strike next. What better source than an established jeweller who, for some reason, had turned to criminal ways? Robert Cooke had warned that many villains were in the gemstone trade. Maybe more than he realised were thriving within the Goldsmith's Guild?

This sent Elizabeth's mind spinning in another whirl of half-guesses and assumptions. But in the absence of anything else, the juxtaposition of the attack to Goldsmith's Row had to be her next line of investigation. It was not possible to ignore it; her need to know would not allow it. But for the first time in her life she was oppressed by fear.

Lost in these thoughts, she almost missed him. A man came into view from the direction of St. Paul's with a cap pulled down to cover his face. He was on the south side of Cheapside and constantly, almost imperceptibly, scanning the street as he walked towards Goldsmith's Row. For the rest of her days, Elizabeth would always remember how her attacker sounded, but she had no idea what he looked like because of his mask, while much of his body had been shrouded in fog. Nevertheless, watching this stranger, there was something in his manner she recognised. This was her man, she was sure of it.

Elizabeth quickly left her position to cross Cheapside. Several market sellers had left their empty stalls along the middle of the street. Robert Cooke would not approve but to Elizabeth they were a blessing, giving her the necessary cover to shadow her man. He was now walking past Goldsmith Row but was showing no interest in the window displays. She faltered and began to doubt her intuition, and when he passed the final shop on Goldsmith's Row and kept walking, her spirits dropped.

Elizabeth was about to give up the chase but there was something about the man that made her keep walking. And then he was gone.

She stopped and stared up and down Cheapside. Her mystery man had disappeared, literally in the blink of an eye. She crossed to the pavement on the south side and started to run. She must not lose him. As she got nearer to where he had been, she saw an opening into an alley on her right.

Her breath shortened as she approached the alley, still running. She had to carry on, but the thought of coming face to face with the man behind the mask, waiting for her as she turned the corner, made her quake. Her hand dipped in to her pocket and, looking around, she took another swig of arrack and replaced the bottle. She gasped and turned right.

The alley was empty, save for some ragged children playing with a ball and stick. The stranger had disappeared. Without warning, she burst into tears, the welling pressure inside released in convulsive sobs. A passer-by looked at her curiously but kept walking. She started to trot down the alley, keeping the side of Goldsmith's Row on her right. She reached the next corner of the building and viewed the surrounding area. She could see clearly in every direction but there was no sign of the stranger. She was certain he had not come this far, and must have entered Goldsmith's at some point. Wearily she turned around and walked past several doors, back towards Cheapside. Should she knock and enquire if a masked attacker lay within? The hopelessness and absurdity of her situation momentarily made her laugh inside, hysterically. She had to get a grip. She was missing Tom badly. She realised with a shock that it was Tom who had stopped her drinking and gambling when they met and, now he was out of her daily life, she had reached for the bottle again.

Every aching fibre in her body told her to give up this hopeless chase, but her instinct and logic demanded she continue. She was convinced the man she pursued must be near, so she found another hiding place, this time near the top of the alley. Fifteen minutes later, she was on the point of giving up when a door opened on the side of Goldsmith's Row and the man slipped out and turned right, walking rapidly away from her. She tried to keep pace for a hundred yards but her body would take her no further. At least she knew where he had been. She carefully approached the door but it was locked tight. She glanced at the window next to it. No sign of light.

What was on the other side of that door? One person would know. Minutes later, she was inside Robert Cooke's office, the jeweller offering her a mug of small beer solicitously. The coal burning in his fireplace was throwing out an intense heat and feeling was returning to Elizabeth's fingers. She was exhausted, but triumphant. She had identified the jewel robber and his location, she was sure of it. Robert Cooke listened carefully to her description of the man and the door he used to enter the building.

'If you followed him down Friday Street, I am not surprised that side of the Row looked deserted. Those offices have been shut for six months. We can't get any goldsmiths to take up a lease. They say it's too expensive when they're no longer required to work from Cheapside.'

'But that cannot be. I saw this man leave through that doorway.'

'Well, that is most unusual. Maybe someone has broken in and now uses it as a store for these thefts? Miss Seymour, it would be wonderful if through your bravery and tenacity you have trapped our robbers! My, my.' Cooke paused, his face glowing with delight. He jumped up out of his seat. 'Well, there's only one way to find out. Please wait while I get a key from the Guild office. We keep one here in case prospective tenants arrive and wish to inspect the property,' and he strode out of the room. Elizabeth basked in the heat from the fire and minutes later Cooke returned, brandishing the key. 'Let us investigate, and maybe catch the robbers in their lair!'

They left the shop and hurried to Friday Street. Cooke was like a little boy on an adventure. 'We must be cautious, Mr. Cooke,' Elizabeth warned. 'If anyone is there, it might be dangerous.'

'Never fear, dear lady. We will take it steady. '

They approached the door and Cooke put his ear to the lock. 'I cannot hear anything. Let us look through the window.' Cooke edged up to the side and peered in. He was some six inches taller than Elizabeth and could get a better view. 'No sign of movement. I think we should use the key. But any sign of trouble and we will retreat immediately.'

Elizabeth nodded. Cooke's face was a study of care. He slowly placed the key in the lock and turned, grunting with the effort. 'I am trying to turn it slowly' he whispered 'but it is quite stiff.' Finally, she heard a click and he eased the door open. Keeping it ajar, Cooke listened again, then slowly opened the door fully. The room was empty and its air smelt musty. He stepped in and strode towards the only door at the back of the room. 'These offices usually have additional rooms in the back' and he opened the door to reveal a small space with two other open doors. There was enough light from the front window for Elizabeth to see these rooms were both empty as well. She turned to Cooke. 'I know what you must think but I'm not mistaken. This was definitely the office he entered. I'm sure of it.'

Cooke avoided her gaze, looking both disappointed and a little embarrassed. 'Of course, my dear lady. I wouldn't doubt it for a second but unfortunately, as you can see, the cupboard is bare!' He attempted a conciliatory smile but seeing Elizabeth's steely expression, thought better of it. In the ensuing silence, the only sound was the rattle of wagons and the cry of hawkers outside the window. London life continued to roll by, only increasing Elizabeth's feeling of helplessness. She had lost her best chance of discovering the jewel thief and her investigation was no further forward.

'Of course, it is possible that your man used this office simply as a secret meeting place…' Cooke suggested.

'…and if I had waited a little longer, after he left, I might have seen his contact depart as well?'

'Well, it would have been logical for the second man to delay his departure, so that they weren't seen together?'

She rolled her eyes with frustration. The second man had probably walked past while she was sitting with Cooke in his office. She was losing patience with the whole affair. Better to give her necklace to Lucy Carlisle with an apology – it was, after all, flawed - and suffer the gossip about Elizabeth Seymour and stolen goods that was bound to follow.

Elizabeth arrived at her parent's house exhausted and defeated. Slipping in through the kitchen entrance, she put her finger to her lips as she tiptoed past the startled cook in her street disguise, before climbing the stairs to her bedroom, and the nightmares to come.

Chapter 27

Syon House, near Brentford

'Are you sure this will work, Barty?'

Tom was peering through a thick clump of bushes at the imposing outline of Syon House, the lights from its windows twinkling in the gathering gloom. Barty scrambled forward and knelt next to him.

'I do not have a better plan. By following the river, we've avoided the King's army so far. With any luck we should now be east of them. Ahead of us lie the Parliamentary defences of London. If you're careful, you should be able to find someone who can take you to Skippon.'

They had found Sam bound and gagged in a pigsty and Tom's battered face had given Barty an idea for a cover story. Should they stumble on a royal patrol, he and Sam were escorting a Parliament spy to the King's camp for further interrogation but had got lost. It was paper-thin and would not withstand much scrutiny but, so far, they had escaped attention as they travelled through Isleworth, arriving now at Syon House.

'My guess is Essex's army will be gathering at Brentford,' Tom said. 'But meeting them would be perilous for you Barty. You might be recognised as one of the peace delegation and tensions are running high. Some hot head might take a pot shot at you, or drag you off for 'questioning'. And I'm not leaving you here alone, between the two armies.'

Barty nodded. 'Thank you, Tom. Much appreciated, but not necessary now we've reached Syon House. This is the home of the Earl of Northumberland who headed the delegation who met the King. It is the greatest good fortune he lives here. We have reached a safe haven.'

Tom gazed at the imposing mansion. Well, they were due some luck. 'Come on Barty. I'm in need of a hot meal and a decent bed.' He stepped from their cover and strode towards the house, approaching through parkland on the riverside.

As they reached Syon House, they saw groups of soldiers passing in and out of its entrance. One was wheeling a small keg of gunpowder in a barrow. Sam halted but Tom tugged his arm. 'Come Sam, do not be alarmed. The Earl is taking sensible precautions, defending his property.' Sam held back. It was clear he was exhausted and scared witless. The explosion at the ship had taken its toll.

'Sam, go and wait behind that large oak. Barty and I will check all is in order and then return for you.' Sam nodded with relief. Barty and Tom walked past the soldiers and through the main entrance. Troopers were everywhere fortifying the house. He could see a small cannon wheeled into one of the back rooms overlooking the river.

'Well Barty, our lordship is talking peace, but clearly preparing for a fight, if he has to!'

His friend had stopped, several steps behind him, a puzzled frown on his face. 'This is most unexpected…'

Tom was distracted by a movement behind Barty's shoulder. It was Appleyard, standing with his back to them, in discussion with another soldier. Tom grabbed Barty's arm and hissed 'follow me', before pushing him from the room, out of Appleyard's sight.

'We've walked into a trap. This house is occupied by Royalist troops. I've seen Appleyard!'

'Oh my! What have I done, leading you here? But remember, I am known in Parliament as a supporter of the King. Let me deal with this man.'

'No, Barty. Appleyard is a hardliner. One mention or sight of me and he'll have you in irons. This is how he asks his questions', and he fingered his swollen eye. 'We must split up. Without me, you can walk out unmolested through the front door. Take Sam and get help from the Earl. Does he know his house is occupied? I will lay low and attempt to escape during the night.'

'But…'

'We've no time to debate this. I can hear somebody coming. Go Barty. Go!' and he pushed his friend back into the room where Appleyard was in conversation. Flustered, Barty tried to turn back but, realising eyes in the room were on him, stopped and walked to the front entrance without a backward glance.

Tom's mind was racing. He must find a quiet corner in the house to lie low for a few hours. Several candles dimly lit the room he had stumbled into. He took one and began to explore, noticing another door next to a fireplace.

After a brief search, it was clear the mansion had no shortage of hiding places for tonight. Remaining undiscovered during the day would be another matter. He discovered a servant's staircase at the end of a corridor and went up to the first floor. He could not see a single light and the noise from the ground floor was all but stilled.

Tom found a bedroom with a locking door, the key in place. He cautiously entered, waited as long as his exhausted body and mind would allow, listening for any noise, before locking the door. He clambered on to the four-poster bed and was asleep within minutes.

Chapter 28

Little Salisbury House

'So you met the King's boys at this battle…what was it called, this place?'

'Edge Hill, my lady, in the county of Warwickshire, although it is also becoming known as Kineton Fight, named after the nearby villages.'

'Quite so. How brave of them to be with their father.'

Or stupid of their father to risk them, Elizabeth thought. She had heard later from William Harvey that a cannon ball had whistled past them in their place of refuge behind the barn. A yard or two to the right and the line of Stuart succession might have been drastically reduced in a moment.

Elizabeth was selective in her account of Edge Hill. She knew the story of the princes would appeal to Lucy far more than a description of the human carnage on the battlefield. She hadn't yet come to terms with this herself and was not ready to share it with anyone, particularly an unsympathetic ear such as Lucy Carlisle. To show disinterest about such suffering would have been too much for Elizabeth to bear.

There was a knock on the salon door and Lucy's servant entered, looking slightly ruffled. He walked towards them more briskly than his usual stately pace. 'Excuse me, your ladyship, but I have received disturbing information. Syon House has been overrun by the King's army.' It was the first time Elizabeth had ever known Lucy at a loss for words. She sat, with her mouth slightly agape, a bemused frown on her face. 'A member of the Earl of

Northumberland's retinue is at the door, my lady. He is seeking his lordship and thought, as he is not at his Syon House residence, he might be with you?'

Lucy had recovered her senses. 'Well, clearly he isn't. Show the man in.' The servant retreated to the door, as a soldier walked past him into the room, bowing deeply towards Lucy.

'Please excuse my manners, my lady, not waiting to be called, but I must locate his lordship immediately. Syon House has been invaded by Royalist troops who are turning it into a fortress!'

'Well my brother's not here. I haven't seen him in over a week, with all this coming and going with the peace talks. Have you tried Parliament?'

'We have a rider on the way as I speak, with others travelling to other likely locations.'

'How do you know this has occurred at Syon?'

'We currently have troops stationed near Brentford in case of further advances by the King eastwards towards the City.'

'I thought both sides had agreed not to engage while peace negotiations continued at Windsor?' Lucy interrupted. Elizabeth noted once again how well informed she was.

'So they had, nevertheless Royalist troops have advanced, so we need to be prepared. Apparently, our forces near Brentford were approached by a slightly disheveled fellow who insisted he must speak to Philip Skippon on a matter of the greatest urgency and importance.'

'Who was this man?'

'A gentlemen named Sir Bartholomew Hopkins, member of Parliament.'

Elizabeth gave a little start. 'Are you all right, my dear?' Lucy inquired.

'I know him. He is a friend of Tom's.'

'Would that be a Tom Tallant, miss?' the soldier enquired.

Elizabeth nodded, a sense of dread welling inside her. On top of everything else, this was too much.

'Sir Bartholomew, a member of his lordship's peace delegation, had visited Syon House not realising it had been captured by the King's troops. When he discovered what was happening, he left immediately to inform his lordship. But he was forced to leave a man behind who is now hiding within Syon House.'

'And that is Tom?'

'I only heard it in passing. My job is to find his lordship. Is the news of this Tallant important?'

Lucy looked over at Elizabeth whose face was pale, her hands clasped tightly in her lap. 'Yes, it is of consequence, but not for your task. I'm afraid I cannot help you locate his Lordship but this news will travel fast. I'm sure he will know soon, if he has not been told yet. You have performed your duty well. My servant will see you out.' The man gave a short bow and marched from the room, the spurs on his feet jangling with each step.

'I must go to Syon House at once,' Elizabeth said.

'Well of course you must. I can arrange transport now. But what do you hope to do when you get there?'

'I don't know. I will think of something.'

'Elizabeth, I always admire the way you deal with such situations. In a strange way we are alike in this regard. I am forced to live on my wits and gossip. For you, it is your knowledge and facts. Logic is what brings you success when others fail, that and your enquiring mind. But even this may be insufficient when you are confronted by a barricaded Syon House, full of armed men. However, I am very pleased, no excited, to tell you that for once, just once, my knowledge may be greater than yours. And this will prove useful.'

'What do you mean?'

'I grew up at Syon and spent many happy summers as a child playing in the house and grounds. Few knew better where to hide from a scolding, or escape unseen when pursued by an angry governess. Leave this to me. You have my word. Young Thomas will be set free.'

Elizabeth was about to protest but saw the logic in Lucy's suggestion.

'Anyway, we haven't completed our conversation, Elizabeth, have we? My sapphire? I assume you have news?'

Elizabeth had been dreading this moment. She was beginning to hope the Countess had been distracted by events at Syon. But when it came to Lucy's possessions, she should have known better. She always had to be at her sharpest to parry the thrusts and feints which were part of any conversation with the Countess, and she was far from that today. What could she say?

Lucy's body stiffened and a familiar coldness came to her face. 'I assume from your silence that you have no news. No progress has been made?'

Elizabeth fell silent and her head dropped. To her astonishment, she felt tears welling in her eyes. No, no, no! Of all things, this was unforgivable stupidity! Lucy Carlisle preyed on people's weaknesses. What was she doing? Why couldn't she stop?

'What's the matter, Elizabeth?' The temperature in the room plummeted. No consoling hand was offered, or comforting tone of voice. 'What have you done, or not done?'

Something snapped inside Elizabeth. All that she valued - a clear mind, a cool consideration of evidence and logic -

was submerged in a red storm of fear, exhaustion, resentment and despair. 'I'll tell you what I have done. I have risked everything for your tiresome sapphire. I have been attacked in the street, had my life threatened and spent weeks trying to find any sort of rhyme and reason in this business!'

She came to, as if from a faint and realised she was standing, shouting and jabbing her finger at the Countess of Carlisle, who had recoiled in her chair, her face consumed with outrage.

'How DARE you talk to me like that…'

Elizabeth's moment of clarity disappeared as she willingly plunged back into her red mist. Her body was screaming for release, and this was it. 'I'll tell you why I dare. I dare because, unlike you, I have seen the results of the plots and intrigues that amuse you and so many others like you. A whisper here, a secret message there, and another hundred mutilated men are brought to my feet, begging, screaming for help, and I cannot provide it!'

Lucy's expression changed to disbelief. 'Seymour. You're raving! What's wrong with you?'

'No, you wouldn't understand, would you? You haven't seen the misery war will bring to this country, and you don't want to know. More important to get your precious sapphire back, even though it's worthless!'

It was Lucy's turn to be lost for words. Her hands gripped the arms of the chair until her knuckles went white.

'Yes, that's right,' Elizabeth continued. What I have discovered is that your prized stone, if it truly is yours, is flawed. It's been repaired to make it sparkle, but it's not the gem you think it is. Maybe you'll lose interest in it now?'

Elizabeth suddenly was completely spent, like the burnt-out rockets she enjoyed making and setting off at home. She looked in dismay at the wreckage of her relationship with Lucy, reflected in her icy stare. Now she just needed a drink, not her first that day. Had that loosened her tongue? She really didn't care anymore. She just wanted to escape - the room, her world, even London. Perhaps she'd go sailing to India with Tom.

'Have you finished?' Lucy's voice was as cold and flat as iron. 'If you think some stranger accosting you in the street excuses that…that outburst, you have no idea how our world works. I don't give a fig for your terror. You are here to do my bidding. There are dozens of the leading courtiers in England who would do anything to get five minutes of my attention and gratitude. Anything! They have told me as much, frequently. And you will be the same. To think I was comparing you to me, earlier. I'm always told I indulge the lesser sort too much. Never again!

'If what you tell me about my sapphire is true, you will find this jewel thief who will provide a perfect replacement. I will not take anything less, from anyone less. The thought that you must complete a task you now so clearly despise will bring me comfort, that and the thief being brought to justice.

'You will obey this command, and woe betide if you don't. In the meantime, I will free your beau from Syon House. Unlike you, I was raised to live by a code of honour and I will keep my word, despite you artfully extracting it from me before admitting your abysmal failure. Tallant has been steadfast in his assistance to Pym that I requested. I cannot blame him for your perfidious nature, just his poor judge in character in getting entangled with the ill-mannered, ungrateful creature you so clearly are.

'And I would counsel you against any plans to the contrary you may be harbouring, if you know what's good for you…and your family.'

Chapter 29

Syon House

Tom awoke slowly. He had slept heavily, exhausted by days without rest or food. He had been woken by the pale sun, quite high in the sky, shining on his face through the bedroom's large window. He realised it must be mid-morning.

He heard shouting and tramping feet inside and outside the house, and a careful peek from the window confirmed more troops had arrived. He watched the deployment of the new arrivals and it slowly dawned on his sleep-fogged brain why they were making such efforts to fortify the mansion.

In the dark, he hadn't realised how close Syon was to the Thames. The Earl of Northumberland possessed an unrivalled view of the river rolling past his grounds. Downriver lay Parliament's troops. Upriver, to the west, the King's army was gathered at Hounslow Heath. Either side could use the Thames for a flanking attack. However, any vessel would have to pass under the gaze of Syon House, and its newly installed guns. More cannon had appeared, dug in and secured in the grounds, pointing at the river. The trap was almost set. Any thought of escape would have to wait. His duty now was to disarm, or at least disrupt, this new Royalist battery.

Now his mind and body was rested, hunger gnawed at his stomach. He opened the bedroom door and listened, before carefully walking along the corridor to the servants' staircase he had used the previous night. He approached the stairwell and again stopped to listen and weigh up his options.

Once on the stairs, he would be visible to any others using them. But should he retreat and spend the day cloistered like a Jesuit priest in the bowels of this enormous house? What if Appleyard had left this morning? No one else knew Tom and he would be able, in theory, to walk straight out the front door, if he took the risk. Even so, it would be dangerous and he would still face a lengthy journey on foot towards the Parliamentary lines. Tom was lightheaded from his lack of food and drink, and it was the aroma of freshly baked bread coming up the stairwell, rather than consideration of the best strategy, that decided his next move.

He descended the first flight cautiously. As he approached the ground floor, two soldiers strode along the corridor in front of him, side by side and deep in conversation. Both passed without a sideways glance. Now he could hear the clatter of pots and pans and the mouthwatering smell of cooked meat. He continued down the stairwell to the cellar. At any moment Tom expected a shout from above, somebody demanding to know his business, and being caught as a spy was a hanging offence. But his only encounter was with a maid carrying a tray, emerging up the steps from the cellar with her head down, and almost colliding with him.

'Careful, there!' Tom called out. 'That's my breakfast.'

The girl jumped but held on to the tray. She mumbled something, bobbing a curtsey. She's terrified, Tom thought. What mistreatment has she suffered? He smiled at her kindly, and then stared at the fresh bread, cheese and beer. 'I have orders for the cook. Leave the tray with me and fetch her.'

'But the food's meant for the soldiers. I'll get skinned alive if I don't take it to them.'

'I'll look after it. Now go quickly. I will meet her at the bottom of these stairs.' The wide-eyed maid needed no second bidding and ran down the steps into the gloom. Tom followed, grabbing food off the tray and stuffing it in his mouth.

He came to a small alley, dimly lit by a number of sconces fixed along the wall, and sat on the floor, devouring the bread, cheese and beer. He heard an irate voice down the passage. A short, strong armed woman appeared in mop cap and apron, the frightened maid in tow.

'If you're here for more grub, you'll have to wait your turn,' and she glanced at the empty tray on the floor. 'Oh, you've helped yourself. Why doesn't that surprise me?' The maid saw the remains of the tray and burst into tears. 'Hush now, you ninny. No harm done.' The cook's words were harsh but Tom also heard compassion in her voice. All the kitchen, from cook to maid, had little control over events this morning. Her antipathy gave him hope and he decided to risk all.

'Mistress, I need your help. I am a friend of the Earl, trapped in his house by this raiding party of Royalists.'

She gave him a hard stare.'How? We weren't aware of any guests in the house when his lordship left for Colnbrook. Who are you?' She pulled them into a corner as two more servants walked from the kitchen carrying trays. They glanced at the cook questioningly and she nodded towards the stairs.

'How do I know this is not a trick, to test my loyalty. We've been warned what will happen if we make trouble.' The cook was wavering. Any second now she might give them up. He desperately needed to convince her he knew the Earl's family. Then it came to him in a flash.

'Lucy Carlisle,' he blurted out. 'I am acquainted with his lordship's sister, Lucy.'

The woman frowned and folded her thick arms across her ample chest. Oh no, have I got this wrong? Tom thought. He wished he'd paid closer attention when Elizabeth had been describing Lucy's family tree. He was sure she'd said the 10th Earl, Algernon, was Lucy's brother, and Lucy used to visit the 9th Earl, her father, in the Tower.

'Who are you, to be so familiar? Lucy indeed!'

Tom sighed in relief. 'Please accept my apologies. It is the urgency of the moment. I would never, of course, address her in such a manner, should she be here.'

Seeing he had never met Lucy Carlisle, he wasn't sure how he would address her, but Elizabeth had told him enough about her looks, clothes and Little Salisbury House, to make his claim to acquaintance credible. 'And of course, I know the Earl. I have observed him outside the House of Lords on a number of occasions.'

'Oh, you'll tell me you're a Lord next, won't you.'

Tom had by now recovered his equilibrium and he was beginning to tire of this troublesome cook. It was time to take the upper hand. 'No, my good woman. I am a humble member of the House of Commons, your Parliament. It brings me into contact with many powerful men in this land. John Pym, for example, is a personal friend.' Pym's was the only name Tom thought she might know.

'Well. In that case…'

'Is there a servant's entrance to the house, to escape?'

'It's guarded. They're not letting anyone leave. And the grounds are filled with the King's men, both front and back. You'll not get past them in daylight.'

'If I can't escape or deliver a warning about the guns, I'll have to stay and create as much mayhem as possible. Mistress, thank you for the food. If you can spare a little more to keep body and soul alive in the coming days, I will not trouble you again.'

The cook nodded and bustled back to the kitchen, returning minutes later with a small cloth parcel bound tight. 'More cheese and bread and a piece of ham. Now disappear before you get me into serious trouble.'

Tom thanked the cook. 'What's your name, mistress, so I can report your kind assistance to her ladyship?'

'It's Joan…now be off with you.'

He ran up the stairs as quietly as possible, past the sound of men talking and receiving orders but, again, it was coming from the centre of the house. When he reached his room, he began to relax. He opened the door and stepped inside. Something was wrong. The room was darker and the curtains had been drawn. The door slammed behind him and a familiar voice called out, as two armed men emerged from the gloom.

'Ah, there you are Tallant. Good of you to return and make my job easier.'

A curtain was opened to reveal Appleyard, pistol in hand. 'Time to take you to my commander,' he sneered. 'You can tell him how you blew up the gunpowder supply he spent months acquiring. That will put him in a good humour.'

Hours later, Tom found himself once again a prisoner, held in a locked store room. The sight of Appleyard had filled him with an unsettling combination of dread and anger. He was taken to see the commanding officer, fearing more punishment, but thankfully it did not materialise. The man was pre-occupied with the defences of Syon House and did not share Appleyard's conviction about Tom's importance. The officer noticed Tom's healing scars and asked Appleyard how he had acquired them, frowning when the sergeant denied any knowledge of them.

'I understand you have been 'questioned' by Sergeant Appleyard but did not reveal any valuable intelligence. Frankly, you are an unwelcome distraction at this time. I suppose there's no point asking you to keep our position secret, if I let you go?' the officer asked with a resigned smile on his face. Tom looked at the floor. 'No, I thought not. The Sergeant wants to string you up from the nearest tree, but that will not happen, you have my word,' and here again he gave Appleyard a hard stare. 'Hopefully, we can use you in any prisoner exchange. I can't spare anyone to guard you, so you will be locked up for now.'

Tom was pushed back into the storeroom, relieved at escaping another beating. Not all the King's army was as ruthless or cruel as Appleyard, a welcome thought. Minutes later, a muffled roar broke the silence, followed by another, then cheering. They were firing the cannon. Perhaps testing their range, or were they engaging with a Parliamentary ship sailing upriver, trying to outflank the King's men?

He paced towards the window and noticed the afternoon light was fading. How long would he remain here? What of Barty? Had he escaped with Sam through the Parliamentary lines into the city? Tom hoped his friend's status as a Member of Parliament had been sufficient to clear the checkpoints, and he had raised the alarm with the Earl. But if a rescue was launched, how would they reach him? He began to share Sam's gloom. His situation looked hopeless.

Eventually he curled up on the floor and, despite the cold, exhaustion overtook him and he dozed off. He drifted in and out of sleep, woken by pangs of hunger. Then he heard the welcome sound of a key turning in the door lock. Perhaps he would be fed, although he craved something to drink the most. Befuddled by exhaustion, he raised himself on one elbow, peering towards the opening door. A figure stepped inside and closed it quietly behind him. Tom did not recognise him. The visitor bent down and started untying the ropes binding his hands.

'What…what are you doing? Who are you?'

‘My name is of no account, and I am setting you free, which I assume you wish me to do, sir?’

‘Yes...yes, of course’. Tom’s mind was racing, but he knew from the man’s deference that he was almost certainly a servant at Syon House. But why was he risking his life to save Tom…unless? ‘Are you here on the Countess of Carlisle’s behalf?’

‘Oh no, sir. I would not claim to be taking her place. No, I am here at her command.’

By now, Tom’s hands were free and he was rubbing his aching wrists. ‘Well, I am in your debt.’

‘T’is nothing, sir. I have known the Countess since she was a young girl. She always got her way with me. Distant memories now in these troubled times. When I received her note, smuggled in from the village, well, it pleased me to know that she remembered me and required my assistance.’

‘But how are we going to escape from the house.’

‘Ah, as the Countess well knows from her games as a child, Syon House is blessed with many excellent hiding places, including a secret passage that runs from the gallery to the grounds outside. I will take you to its entrance and my friend from the village will be waiting for you at the other end, to guide you away from the King’s troops.

‘Just to confuse matters, sir, you should know there are two Brentfords, both on the road leaving London for Bristol. You must head for New Brentford which I’m told marks the front of the Parliamentary defences. Further east of this, heading towards London, is Old Brentford.

‘Now, we must be on our way, as quiet as church mice…and may God give you success, sir. Oh, I almost forgot - when you arrive in New Brentford, someone will be waiting for you. You need to ask the men on duty for a Mr. Nicholas Culpeper. Apparently, he will look after you from there on.’

Tom's heart sank. He knew Culpeper and in his mind he was not to be trusted. He was probably the last person he would want to help him in such circumstances, but Elizabeth believed in him.

The servant was as good as his word and he escaped the house without incident. The villager took him north, constantly watching for Royalist soldiers patrolling the land in between. Tom gathered his remaining strength and prayed for a safe passage. He wasn't sure he could endure capture again and another beating. For once, his prayers were answered. The villager's local knowledge brought them unscathed to the village of New Brentford. But his rising spirits were doused by the familiar sight of Culpeper standing by a barricade erected across the main road to repel the King's expected assault. He was a leading figure among the Coleman Street puritan radicals and Tom was not surprised to see him in Brentford inspecting the defences, shrouded in tobacco smoke from the ever-present large pipe clenched between his teeth.

He and Elizabeth had a firm friendship started by their shared devotion to tobacco. Tom was unnerved by the playful conversation they indulged in and, try as he might, he did not trust the man. He was ashamed to admit he resented their closeness and it made him feel vulnerable, despite Elizabeth's reassurances they were good friends, and nothing else. Culpeper sensed this and was fond of baiting him.

'Tallant! What brings you to the front line of our defences. Not spying for the King, are you?'

'That's enough, Culpeper. I would have you know I have been working for Pym and Skippon, and have suffered greatly at the hands of the King's soldiers as a result.'

Culpeper grunted and carefully knocked out the burnt tobacco from the bowl of his pipe. 'Well, if you're aiding

Pym and Skippon, I will not ask you why, or to what end, as I'm sure the fewer people who know the better. If you want to get back to London, the line of defences surrounding the city are nearing completion and you will find it easier to pass through them in my company.'

'Are they impressive?'

'I hope so, after all the blasted noise they've been making. Work has been non-stop on the section close to my home. Morning, noon and night. Haven't had a good night's sleep in weeks.'

'I need to speak to Philip Skippon, as a matter or urgency,' Tom said.

'I can get you through the lines back into London, but you'll not be able to return if you can't find him there. I've heard talk he's organising the defences of Old Brentford down the road, just like we are here' and he pointed the stem of his pipe to a swarm of red coated soldiers busy blockading the bridge into the town with whatever they could get hold of. 'But I cannot be certain.'

Tom faced a dilemma. If he returned to London but could not locate Skippon, he would have to report to John Pym, and that could take days. And if Skippon's soldiers were manning the barricades in New and Old Brentford, it made sense that he would still be in this area. He turned to Culpeper. 'I will remain here and find the Commander.'

'We expect the action to be hot around Brentford, and you could be trapped if the King attacks and you're on the wrong side of the city's defensive wall.'

'Well, I'll be in good company with the Trained Bands. They looked a formidable group when I saw them going through their paces at Finsbury. There will be safety in their numbers.'

Culpeper was about speak but thought better of it. He looked Tom up and down and smiled. 'Well, that's your decision, Tallant, and I wish you good luck. I will tell

Elizabeth you are alive and well, if I see her. You're always on her mind, you know. Make sure you return in one piece. She needs you.' and, at this, Nicholas Culpeper extended his arm and gripped Tom's hand tightly, tilting his head foreword in acknowledgement.

Chapter 30

Cheapside

Elizabeth sat in Robert Cooke's office watching her host pace the floor. No limp today. The gout must have improved.

Whenever Cooke's back was turned she rubbed her knees gently. Minutes earlier she had fallen face-first on the stone pavement outside Goldsmith's Row. A number of concerned passers-by helped her to her feet but she had politely declined any further assistance. Now she wasn't so sure. The numbing effect of the brandy in her body was wearing off and her knee was starting to ache. But she had bigger worries to face.

'What am I to do, Mr. Cooke?' Elizabeth did not like the tone of her voice. Helpless, almost wheedling. She loathed others speaking that way. What was happening to her?

'I can see your problem, Miss Seymour. The Countess now requires a replacement for her flawed sapphire, an identical replacement, you say?'

Elizabeth just nodded. She didn't want to hear another word of her pleading.

'Well, she will have to accept that's not possible. No two stones are identical. Any jeweller will tell her that. I can keep an eye open for something similar which in itself would be a handsome gemstone, but identical? No, I don't think so.'

'Can you improve the repair to her stone, so that she doesn't notice it?'

'Well, it would appear she wasn't aware of the existing work when the sapphire was in her possession. But if she's now looking for flaws, whatever you give her will be expertly checked. And, good as my work is, it would not fool anyone who knew what to look for. Cooke paused. 'Are you in pain, Miss Seymour? You do not seem comfortable in your chair.'

Elizabeth looked a little embarrassed. 'To tell the truth, Mr. Cooke, I took a bit of a tumble in the street as I was approaching Goldsmith's Row. Lost my footing…'

'My dear lady, I am so sorry. I have been telling the Guild for months to keep the pavement in good order. We cannot have esteemed visitors such as yourself coming to harm. Are you experiencing pain?'

Her right knee was now throbbing. It would be blue in the morning. 'Not at all. Just a little discomfort. Nevertheless, a small restorative draught would be welcome.'

'Perhaps a glass of beer?'

'I was thinking of something a little stronger, Mr. Cooke.'

'Oh, of course, dear lady. My apologies. Now let me see…' and Robert Cooke rose to his feet and started rooting in a cabinet behind his desk, while continuing his conversation. 'As I was saying, I will look for a gemstone of equal size and lustre and unimpeachable quality, but the market is surprisingly quiet at the moment.'

'What do you mean?

'Ah, here's what I was looking for, a bottle of fifteen year old Armagnac, a gift from a grateful Dutch client. They buy much of the best brandy from Gascony, you know.' He came back to Elizabeth with two glasses and the bottle which he placed on a small table in front of them.

'Now, where was I? Yes, the market. It's very quiet. I fear it is due to the recent robberies. I can see no logic behind them. The thieves steal large hauls – private collections, or from jewellers and their suppliers, the merchants. This creates a scarcity which increases demand for gemstones.

However, any jewel of quality coming to the market in the foreseeable future will be studied closely to establish whether it's from a stolen collection. Even the provenance of loose, raw stones will be questioned. Which is why the Goldsmith's Guild has been unable to trace any sales of highly valuable jewels in recent months. The robbers appear to be sitting on them, which is dangerous and wasteful for characters like the man who attacked you, Miss Seymour. In our experience, thieves like him sell their plunder as soon as possible.

Elizabeth was eyeing the bottle, hoping Cooke would notice. She gave a gentle cough.

'Oh, forgive me. I'm such a thoughtless host. Your drink, of course…' and he uncorked the Armagnac and poured Elizabeth a generous measure. She put the deep amber liquid to her lips and the rich smell of the brandy enveloped her like balm. She took a careful, but prolonged, draught and sat back, letting the warmth wash through her body. It was the best she had ever tasted.

'Thank you, Mr. Cooke. This is most restorative. But unfortunately it does not get me any further with my investigation. There is not a replacement stone in sight, and I have Lucy Carlisle's other condition to fulfill – to catch the robber. Usually by this stage, some revealing pattern has emerged, but not this time. I feel in need of inspiration,' and, at this, she swallowed another mouthful of the blessed Armagnac.

'One possible clue is the sapphire that started this whole affair. I tend to believe Lucy's story that it was stolen from her and then emerged on the market for my father to buy for me.'

'Yes, probably because it is flawed, and so of little use to the thieves,' Cooke concurred.

'This would have been their one mistake, if only the shop where my father purchased the jewel was still open, but the owner has disappeared. I did think the robberies might be another form of warfare between the King's side and their Parliamentary enemies.' Elizabeth continued. 'But I've checked all the victims. Some are Royalist. Some are, I was surprised to discover, Puritan…' at this Cooke nodded knowingly, 'and some are neither.'

'And why steal so much?' Cooke interjected. 'Amassing a hoard of rings, chains, brooches, and gold. For what purpose? They dare not sell individual items in case they're discovered as the source. If they were desperate, they could dump them all on the market simultaneously. This would create enough chaos, for enough time, to allow the thieves to make some quick coin and then disappear in the confusion. But the price of gold and gems would collapse in such a glut. In the end, they would only get a fragment of their true worth.'

'I did have one theory,' Elizabeth ventured. 'You may know the Queen is currently in the United Provinces.'

'Yes, I believe she's in The Hague, looking after Princess Mary.'

'Well that may be so, but she has also taken a number of the Crown Jewels to buy arms for the King's cause.'

Cooke looked shocked. 'But their majesties are merely custodians of the royal jewels. Too break up such a collection is…is unthinkable!'

Elizabeth smiled at Cooke's naivety. 'Needs must, Mr. Cooke. May I?' She was tilting her empty glass towards the bottle and the jeweller, eager to be privy to more royal news, hurried to replenish it.

'You see, the King is lacking the resources to raise an army,' Elizabeth continued. However, I can assure you the jewels we seek have not taken a similar route. I have it from the highest authority that no other collections have been sent to The Hague to generate funds.'

'You learned that from the Countess?'

'No, no…much higher than that, although she was the messenger.' Elizabeth was enjoying demeaning Lucy's role. She once would have thought it beneath her but now, she had to admit, it amused her.

'No, from higher, close to the Queen herself. So, sadly that avenue of enquiry has been proven to be a false trail.' The room fell silent and Elizabeth noticed it was starting to sway, just a little. Good. Life was much more bearable like this.

There was a knock on the shop door and Robert Cooke rather guiltily sprung from his seat to answer it. Silly man. He's embarrassed to have a young woman alone with him in his office, plying her with drink. Maybe he does have another motive? She giggled but then refocused. No, he's silly, but harmless. Her drunken mind lurched in a contrary direction. Not like the masked man. He's not harmless.

Cooke was now standing in his workshop, near the front door, and snatches of conversation with his visitor drifted into her consciousness as she thought for the fiftieth time about her encounter with her attacker, replaying it over and over.

The visitor suddenly raised his voice, laughing. Elizabeth frowned as her mind slid into a warm bath of deep amber Armagnac. As ever, Cooke's fire was blazing. He knows how the build a good fire, Mr. Cooke. Nightmares from Kineton preyed on her mind most nights and now she felt herself drifting into a restful half-sleep.

The man laughed again. He was shouting something. Oh, go away Mr. Visitor. Leave me in peace.

'You'll be the talk of every pub in London, Mr. C!..the talk of every pub!'

What's the man saying? Elizabeth's mind was swimming between the voice in her head…no, between two voices in her head. 'The talk of every pub'…they're both saying the same thing. How can that be? That second voice is Masked Man. He didn't say anything like that when he attacked me…'

Elizabeth's eyes opened wide, and her body sat bolt upright. The glass fell from her hand and smashed on the floor. She heard herself shouting. 'No. No. It can't be..' then fell in a dead faint.

She opened her eyes minutes later to see the harassed face of Robert Cooke staring over here. 'Oh thank goodness, Miss Seymour. What happened to you? I heard you shout just as my visitor was leaving and then the sound of broken glass. I came in from the workshop and found you collapsed in your chair.

Elizabeth pulled herself upright. Her head was thumping but, to Robert Cooke's surprise, she was smiling. 'I've got him, Robert. I know who my attacker is. And with that knowledge, we'll find the jewels, you can be sure of it.'

'I don't understand what you are saying.'

'It's your visitor. I have your visitor to thank.'

'Silas? How did he help? He's always pestering me with bits of paste he's bought, convinced they're worth a fortune. I humour him because he's a lonely widower with a small amount of money and it keeps him happy to dream.'

'Of being the talk of every pub in London?'

Cooke smiled. 'Yes, for Silas, that would be a dream fulfilled, In this case he was assuring me I would also share that acclaim if I would just tell him that his pieces of painted glass were prime rubies. But what of it?'

'After I was confronted by the masked man, I had the strongest feeling I had heard his voice before. It was not familiar, but I'd heard a snatch of it at some time. I tried to put the thought out of my head until I heard Silas saying you could be the talk of every pub. And that's when I remembered. It was a phrase I had heard before from the robber.'

'While he was threatening you in the alley? That seems a strange thing to say.'

'No. That's just it. It was something I had heard him shout to his gang, almost a year ago when they had attacked the warehouse of my good friend Thomas Tallant. I had arrived there with soldiers from the Trained Bands to intervene and heard him shout this out. It was just a snatch but enough to make his voice familiar.'

Cooke looked expectantly at Elizabeth. 'And if this is to help, you must know this man?'

'Oh yes, I know him all right. I know Billy Boy, and now I have him in my sights. Tom will find him, and will be only too glad to do so. And from Billy, it will be a short step to apprehending our jewel thief.'

Chapter 31

West of New Brentford

Tom sat in the yard of a large house, his frustration mounting. His earlier relief at escaping Syon House was now turning to anger. Culpeper had secured him a bed in New Brentford and he awoke the next morning, revived and eager to find Philip Skippon. He was told to walk westwards towards the enemy lines until he reached the Trained Band's most forward position at the house of local noble Sir Richard Wynn. But Skippon was not there. Just a group of suspicious troopers who placed him under arrest.

'I would not wish to be in your shoes when it's discovered you have delayed my message.'

His guard yawned and got down on his haunches, facing Tom. 'Look. You've appeared on the road, out of nowhere, asking to speak to some Philip Skippon, who I've never heard of, and you can't tell me who my real commanding officer is. Hereabouts is crawling with Royalist scouts, spies and skirmishers. My money is you're one of them, so I'm sure you'll be seen when the officers have time, but they're otherwise occupied at the moment, building our defences. So stay where you are, and shut your mouth, before I lose my patience.'

Tom surveyed the surrounding countryside. The early morning fog from the river was lingering. How well could this position be defended? Much of the land nearby had been enclosed. The hedges bordering the roads from Wynn House were now shedding their leaves and would not provide as much cover as the Parliamentary soldiers hoped.

A group of mounted soldiers were approaching. The guard peered over the hedge and shouted towards the house. 'Stand lively. Officers approaching.' This prompted a stir of activity as the leading figure in the group entered the yard. Tom's heart leapt. He knew this man.

'Mr. Holles? Denzil Holles? I must speak to you on a matter of grave importance.'

The guard cuffed him on the side of his head, grabbing his arm. 'Be quiet, or I'll have you locked up.'

Tom ignored him. 'Mr. Holles. I am Thomas Tallant, a fellow member of Parliament. We have met before.'

The rider stopped and leaned forward in his saddle, peering at Tom. 'No…no, I don't believe I know you, sir,' and pulled on his horse's reins to ride back to the other mounted men.

'I am Thomas Tallant…I interrupted a speech in the Commons by crossing the floor of the house to give John Pym a message. Don't you remember? The message which saved you from arrest by the King.'

Tom would never forget that day: the note he received from Elizabeth for Pym's urgent attention; the expression on Holles's face, sitting next to Pym, when he interrupted an important speech to the house by leaving his bench to cross the floor to Pym; the congratulations from puritan MPs when they realised his message had saved Pym from imminent arrest by the King; and the fact that, throughout, he had no clue what he was doing, or what was in the note. Yes, he remembered it clearly and now prayed Holles recalled it as well.

Holles stopped and swiftly dismounted. 'Trooper, release this man. Let him come to me.' For the first time in days, Tom dared to hope his news would reach the right ears, hopefully in time to wreck the plans of the royal troops.

Holles looked him up and down and clicked his fingers. 'I have it now, yes. I was not best pleased when I saw you creeping towards Mr. Pym and I, across the floor, like a barn rat. Most irregular. But your warning saved us from the King's clutches, where I would probably still be but for your intervention. So, I am in your debt sir. How can I help you, and what brings you here?'

Tom ushered him to a private corner in the yard. 'I urgently need to speak to Philip Skippon about a confidential but urgent matter. However I also have news of the King's troops and their positions, which I can share with you. They have captured the Earl of Northumberland's home at Syon House and the main army is assembling at Hounslow Heath. I fear they are readying themselves for an attack.'

'I think you are mistaken. The King has agreed to cease hostilities while Parliament considers peace terms. Skippon is in London, as we speak.'

Tom cursed. He had guessed wrong, but nothing could be done about that now. 'So how many men do you have to defend the whole of Brentford? A thousand? More? Less?'

'That's my business Tallant. Anyway, it's not a concern because the King has retired to Windsor to await out our peace terms.'

'If that is so, why have his soldiers not joined him? Instead they are camped just west of here on the Heath.'

'I am beginning to question the value of your intelligence, Tallant. I doubt what you say and why should they capture Syon House? It is of little value to the King if he decides to march on London. It lies too far south, below New Brentford, next to the….river…'

Tom saw the light of realisation in Holles's eyes. 'Yes, the Thames. The Parliamentarians have mounted cannon in the grounds near the riverbank, controlling the waterways from Isleworth to Kew. If they wish, they can now outflank you with men and supplies and stop you doing the same.'

Holles said nothing. He bent down and plucked a long stem of grass from the ground rolling it in his fingers. 'What you say about Syon is interesting, but I'm more concerned at the moment about our defences here, and the enemy's position. You expect Rupert and his cavalry to come charging down the road from Hounslow at any moment?'

'I cannot be sure, but I suggest you prepare for that eventuality.'

'We have scouts on the road but it's hard to find anything in this damn fog. God forbid that whoreson is heading our way. My men have seen enough of him.'

Tom studied Denzil Holles. In Parliament, he had been among the King's fiercest opponents, but now he appeared somewhat reduced. Mixing with his redcoats that morning, Tom had heard how they'd taken the full force of Rupert's cavalry charge at Edge Hill. The loss of life had been dreadful. 'How many men do you have after the Kineton Fight?'

'No more than eight hundred, and they suffer still from the memory of so many comrades cut down. We've filled the gaps with apprentices but they are raw. We will do our duty but I fear for the regiment if they face Rupert again. I thought one great battle would decide this war, bring the King back to his senses. Now I doubt it, and the thought of Englishmen continuing to hack each other to pieces because their leaders cannot find an accommodation…well, I am now less certain I have the stomach for it.'

Tom was shocked. The carnage at Edge Hill must have been appalling to effect such a change in a Parliamentary zealot like Denzil Holles. And now his men would again be in the front line of Parliament's defence of London.

'How soon can you get reinforcements?'

'You are full of questions, Tallant. Why should I share such information when, for all I know, you might be in the King's pay, spying on our positions?'

'Mr. Holles, if I was for the King why would I have alerted you, John Pym and the three other MPs about the King's intent to arrest you?' Tom held his breath. If Holles knew that, at the time, he had no idea what the note contained, all would now be lost. He'd be thrown in prison as a King's spy.

Holles paused, looking at the hurried efforts to build defences around the house, and finally nodded his head. 'You are right. It would be a strange thing for a royal spy to do, making himself known to a full House of Commons. No, there are no reinforcements available at present, although we have another four hundred of Brooke's men back in Old Brentford, with some of Hampden's greencoats in reserve. I will inform the other commanders about Syon House but stay close Tallant. If you're seen running towards the enemy's positions, I'll have you shot, without question.'

Tom swallowed hard. Royalist forces to the west and Holles' suspicious and nervous troops to his right, fingering the trigger on their muskets, waiting for the order to fire, at anyone. He still needed to report to Skippon about the gunpowder smuggling. But currently that was impossible and, anyway, it had been overtaken by events. He was needed here. Every additional man would count and, having been assured by Holles a message would be sent to Skippon immediately, he was issued with a musket, sword and pistol and a small amount of shot and powder.

'We're desperately short of ammunition,' Holles disclosed. 'We will have to scour New Brentford for more. Wynn's house is a trap for my men if we defend it too heavily. They would eventually be surrounded. So we will place musketeers at all windows facing west, with orders to withdraw when capture is imminent and join others hidden either side of the road to New Brentford. Light cannon have been installed behind these hedges to discourage any cavalry attack.

'We will hold this ground for as long as possible, then fall back to the first barricade, on the narrow bridge over the river Brent. You will be stationed there with others, providing covering fire for the men withdrawing from Wynn's house. Both the bridge and the surrounding banks have been strongly barricaded and should provide an effective obstacle.

'If the bridge is overcome, our final barrier to the King's advance is further east, down the London Road, on the approach to Old Brentford town, where there is a slight rise, to give us at least a small advantage against our attackers. It's imperative we hold our ground as long as possible. The entire artillery of the Parliamentary army is currently assembled on the other side of Old Brentford, near Turnham Green, awaiting orders, and the guns are only lightly protected.'

'Why has it been left so vulnerable to capture?

'Because we believed hostilities had ceased while peace talks occurred. It appears we have been much too trusting of this King.'

Chapter 32

New Brentford

Tom stood behind the barricade, peering into thick mist. Somewhere, ahead of him, he could hear the King's attack on Wynn's house. The push for London was underway. Only fourteen hundred foot soldiers stood in the King's way - Holles men backed by around six hundred of Lord Brooke's purple coats, waiting further back in Old Brentford.

The crackle of musket fire drifted through the fog, punctuated by the occasional roar of a cannon. Men were cheering and shouting. 'Sounds like they've repelled the King's cavalry.' It was the captain commanding the barricade, who was standing next to Tom.

'I don't think they will give up so easily,' Tom replied.

'This is not cavalry country, because of the enclosed fields and hedges. They have to attack on a narrow front, along the lane to the house. Once the men and horses in the van are brought down by the cannon, there's no way through. It'll be the infantry's job to slog it out. But the King's got plenty of them waiting.'

Tom looked at the hundreds of redcoats manning the barricade. They were set, muskets loaded and swords sharpened, crouched behind a pile of felled trees, old barrels and broken furniture. All chatter had stopped when the distant gunfire started, their gaunt faces now staring silently into the mist.

Many were praying, one or two older men whispering words of encouragement to white faced boys standing next to them. The survivors of Edge Hill were steadying the newly recruited Apprentice Boys, but what horrors were they pushing from their own memory? The soldiers looked like a goodly number to defend such a small outpost, but it would soon be swamped by a tide of Royalist infantry.

A single figure appeared from the mist, running towards the bridge. A musket shot rang out from Tom's right but the soldier kept on running. 'Hold your fire!' the captain screamed. 'He's a redcoat, one of ours!' The man stumbled towards them. 'Let him through…and I'll hang the next man who fires before my command. We're precious few to be killing each other' he muttered as the soldier arrived, breathing heavily.

'We have withdrawn from Sir Richard Wynn's House as ordered, sir. We beat off the cavalry and they held back awhile. Eventually, large numbers of their foot soldiers advanced through the hedges and around our flanks. We retreated from the position to save as many men as possible. But not before we gave Prince Rupert a bloody nose.' This last comment drew a cheer from the men at the barricade. As he spoke, more redcoats appeared through the mist in two and threes, carrying their muskets, running full pelt to the bridge.

'Let them all through, then close the barricade and take up your positions. Pikemen to the rear.' the captain shouted. The men lined up, the musketeers three deep with a phalanx of pikemen behind them. It will be an unwelcome sight for the approaching King's troops, but how would it withhold the sheer weight of Royalist numbers?

The captain looked at the faint image of the sun, lightening a circle of grey cloud blanketing the sky. 'The defenders at Wynn's house have delayed the King's advance by close to an hour and we are approaching mid-day. With God's grace, we may yet save the artillery.' Time was of the essence. The November days were getting shorter and the King would be unable to press home his advantage in the dark. There was a shout ahead and a final figure emerged from the mist still swirling in the air.

'It's Sergeant Eyre. Make way. He'll be the last one out.' The man flung himself through the closing gap in the blockade and bent over, hands on knees, breathing deeply.'

'Is the road ahead now clear of our men, Sergeant?'

The man straightened up. 'Yes, captain. We have saved more than we lost and those are with you now. But we are grievous low on shot and powder, sir.'

'I have men scouring New Brentford. They have orders to keep the peace but brook no argument if they discover arms we can seize. Sergeant Eyre, this is Thomas Tallant who is a late arrival to our party. I believe this will be his first taste of action. Please will you guide him in our ways. I believe you have something in common as you are both held in Philip Skippon's regard.'

Before Tom could protest, Sergeant Eyre stepped forward and shook his hand vigorously. His broad, open face broke into a ready smile and Tom took to him immediately. He radiated confidence and competence, two attractive qualities in their current situation. 'We must talk of Philip later. But we will have company soon, so let's take up our positions and say our prayers. Andrew, George, Joseph. Stand by me.'

Three men approached. 'Master Thomas! What are you doing here?'

'Andrew. You're a sight to behold!'

The two embraced. Tom turned to Sergeant Eyre. 'Before he joined the Trained Bands, Andrew worked in my warehouse as groom to my horse.'

Eyre nodded, smiling. 'Andrew joined us after Edge Hill; to defend London, he said. Well, you've got your wish, Andrew lad. You'll have plenty of defending to do in the next few days! You'll both have time to catch up once we're in position. Let's get onto the bridge.'

Together they took their stand behind the barricade on the bridge's right hand side. Ahead, the river's northern bank was lined with more Parliamentary troops, around a cannon pointing up the road, with another on the south bank. Together they would rake the king's army on both sides with deadly effect, as it approached the barricade.

'Let's settle ourselves here' Sergeant Eyre called out, 'where the action will be hot, I think.'

'Sergeant! Look.' George was pointing at a group of horsemen emerging from the mist at walking pace. They stopped and surveyed the defences before withdrawing into the fog.

'The forward guard of Prince Rupert's cavalry. We can expect more.'

The gun crews readied themselves, re-sighting their cannon and bringing their small store of ammunition closer. There's not enough, thought Tom, and they won't find any cannon balls in Brentford.

'George, Joseph and I…we battled together, shoulder to shoulder, at Kineton Fight. They know what to expect and won't be found wanting. It's the new arrivals, the Apprentice Boys like Andrew who I worry about. But he seems willing enough.'

'He's a good lad but a bit raw. I'm glad he's got you to keep an eye on him. Kineton must have been a terrible experience.'

'Aye, we lost too many. Honest, god-fearing men, committed to ending the oppression of this King and his lackies like Bishop Laud. The Lord has seen fit to test us, and will do so again, until we achieve his victory.'

Sergeant Eyre dropped his head and Tom realised he was praying. The whole barricade was now silent, waiting in expectation and dread. The only sound was the flow of water from the River Brent as it passed under the bridge and a group further up the line singing a popular psalm. Tom closed his eyes for a moment and pictured walking with Elizabeth along a riverbank as she searched for healing wild plants.

Then he heard. A low rumble, getting louder. The sound of hooves drumming on the ground. Phantoms at full gallop.

'Stand by, men.' It was the captain, shouting along the line. 'Muskets primed and ready!' At this, the redcoats shouldered their guns and aimed down the road, into the fog. The unreality lasted a second more before a dozen horsemen burst through the mist, swords drawn, yelling and screaming.

'Take aim! Steady! Wait for my command.' The captain shouted his orders above the rising cacophony as the cavalry thundered towards the bridge. Each second brought them closer. The ground shook under Tom's feet. He could see the horses, eyes wild and mouths slathering on the bit. For god's sake, give the order before we are over-run!

'Fire!', the captain screamed and Tom's world disappeared into a nightmare of flame, choking smoke and men and horses screaming. He braced himself for the impact. But as the smoke cleared he saw the front rank's charge had been reduced to a tangle of riders and horses, blocking the lane. Some lay dead as others struggled to remount badly injured steeds. A cavalry officer staggered to his feet and, examining his mount, dispatched him with a single shot before limping back to the Royalist lines. Another horse was thrashing its rear legs pitifully.

Tom's ears were singing from the roar of the nearby cannons and, as his head cleared, the mournful sound of the wounded – man and beast - became clearer. The charge had been brought to a complete stop, as had the infantry advance behind it. A second cavalry attack would be impossible.

'They didn't commit enough men to the first charge. The road was too narrow.' Eyre said, his voice professional, matter of fact. 'We've chosen our position well. They've got a job on to winkle us out.'

Eyre's voice broke through Tom's dazed fascination with the bloody scene in front of him. Then he noticed his musket had not fired. Frowning, he examined the priming pan.

'Not discharged?' Eyre asked. 'They're giving us rubbish to fight with. If we get a moment, I'll check if it's beyond repair. It might only need a good clean.'

'Hold your fire.' It was the captain again. 'Let them clear their dead and wounded.'

Tom was impressed by the discipline of the redcoats. Mauled at Edge Hill, he expected many would be thirsting for revenge but the captain had them firmly under control. The surviving cavalry staggered back to the lines, now visible through the disappearing fog. A fortunate few still had their horses. Cautiously others advanced to help the wounded and retrieve the dead. A shot rang out as another horse was put out of its misery.

Eyre turned to Tom. 'Come, let me look at your musket. There'll be no fighting for a while now.' And so it proved. The Royalist cavalry had tested the Parliamentary defences and received a bloody nose. They held their ground awaiting new orders, while the redcoats reloaded their weapons and waited.

The King's army filled the road, out of range of the muskets on the barricade. One or two excited troopers fired at them and were sharply reprimanded by the captain. 'Hold your fire! Save your ammunition until it can be of use.'

'Got your breastplate bright and polished, Andrew? The captain will be along soon to inspect it.' The comment from

Joseph brought laughter from the soldiers around them and a playful kick aimed by a bashful Andrew.

'Andrew is strapped into a piece of armour worn by his father in the German wars. His mother insisted he brought it with him,' Eyre commented smiling. 'They make no end of sport with him.'

The men settled down to wait. Time was on their side. Tom judged it was early afternoon with not many hours of light left. The King needed to renew the attack quickly and it did not surprise him when he saw movement ahead. Dozens of Royalist musketeers were running forward, crouching down, and taking up positions behind the bodies of the fallen cavalry horses.

Seconds later a ragged volley of fire came from their ranks. A man near Tom called out and fell to the floor. He lay on his back, dead, blood flowing from his face. Several more redcoats keeled over and again fire was returned from the defences.

'Heed my orders, damn you,' the captain screamed, real anger in his voice. 'Save your powder and shot until I tell you to fire.'

'Keep your heads down men!' Sergeant Eyre shouted to the troopers around him. Sit tight and don't give them a target. You'll get your chance soon enough.'

He turned to Tom. 'This is the hard time, waiting to be shot. They know they've got the men, so they'll try to wear us down.' Yes, but they don't have the time, Tom thought again, and he saw more musketeers joining them on the lane.

Tom was kneeling behind a broken pew and he thanked the Lord for the protection it offered. The fire from the King's forward positions was close enough to hit the barricade but rarely landed where intended. He ducked as shots thudded into the pew. Musket balls whistled overhead as the air filled with acrid gunpowder smoke drifting from the Royalist positions. There was nothing to be done but crouch as low as possible, musket in hand, and pray. The volleys of shots were increasing and, above the noise Tom heard the advancing soldiers getting closer.

Joseph cried out in pain and fell to his knees, holding his face. 'I've been hit, oh mother and father, I've been hit!' Sergeant Eyre scrabbled across to Joseph's position and pulled his bloodied hands away from his face.

'Let me see…you'll live. A splinter in your cheek. Sit still,' and he pulled a shard of wood out of Joseph's face. 'The captain will have to make his move soon.'

Tom found a small gap in the barricade and risked a peek. He was alarmed to find the Royalist infantry, emboldened by the absence of return fire had now filled the lane and were steadily walking closer to their position.

'Another ten yards…'

Musket balls were now relentlessly pounding their position. Tom was in a state of paralysis. His only wish was to dig a deep hole and disappear from this hell.

'Men, be ready!' Somehow he heard the captain's voice over the constant sound of gunfire.

'On my command, take aim and fire'.

Tom looked at Sergeant Eyre in horror. Raising his head above the barricade to find a target was unthinkable. Exposing any part himself to the storm of lead sweeping over them contradicted his current overwhelming instinct for survival.

He regarded the others and saw fear, but also determination.

'Take careful aim, then fire at will.' The captain bellowed.

Tom said a prayer and lifted his gaze. Within seconds two more redcoats near him crumpled to the floor. He desperately tried to keep his concentration. He sighted three Royalist soldiers, standing close to each other. One was aiming, the other two reloading. At this range, surely he would hit one of them. He breathed in, pulled the trigger and, this time, the musket kicked into his shoulder as it fired. He didn't wait for the smoke to clear and dived for cover as returning fire from the King's infantry whistled past his face. His mind was racing. He had never shot at a man before. Did he hit one of his targets? What if the man was dead?

'Reload, Tom! Reload!'

Sergeant Eyre was bent over a fallen redcoat, shouting at Tom. It was Andrew, knocked on his back by a musket ball to his chest. Tom fumbled with his powder and shot, his mind in a whirl. Had Andrew been killed? And what of the man he had aimed at?

He heard another volley of shots from the bridge and cries from the Royalist line. The frequency of incoming fire faltered and then stopped.

'Hold your fire, men.'

Tom dared to peek over the shredded remains of his pew. His heart dropped when he saw a figure lying on the ground where his target had been standing. Did his shot kill him? Was he young? Old? The lane ahead was a scene of grim chaos. The road was littered with corpses of men to add to the remains of the cavalry horses. Once again they were removing the dead and wounded to clear a path for the advancing army.

Tom saw with relief that Andrew was sitting up, but looking groggy. 'We've done well, so far,' Sergeant Eyre said. 'More time used up, but we must be ready to withdraw sharpish,' he said.

'But we're holding our ground!'

'Their next assault will be a mass attack. As I say, they have the troops and can't afford any further delay. We'll get the order to start a withdrawal to the next line of defences soon.' As he spoke, Tom noticed a wagon full of wounded redcoats set off down the road behind them towards London. Looking forward, he saw the body of the man he'd shot at had also been removed. Was he alive? Tom doubted it. Another victim to add to the dozens that day. Tom would never know, yet never forget him.

'Look sarge, look!' It was Andrew, pointing at his chest and a small dent in his breastplate. 'Aye, you can all have your fun, but that's saved me, it has!' They clapped him on the back, the tension released, and Sergeant Eyre gave him a nudge. 'Your mother wouldn't have another of those, would she?'

A shout went up. 'Here they come again!' and Tom barely had time to take position behind the battered pew before a mass of infantry came into view walking steadily down the lane, four or five deep. It was indeed a mass attack.

He expected the command once again to hold fire, but it didn't come. With so many infantrymen approaching, wasting their precious ammunition was no longer an issue. Fire into the mass of troops and they couldn't miss. With so little room to manoeuvre the battle had been reduced to an attritional game of numbers. Their first volley would be deadly but the remaining Royalists would be upon them before most had time to reload.

The reassuring voice of the captain rang out again. While his orders endured, so would their discipline, and hope. 'Men, let's be at them. Take aim. Fire!'

Again the roar of cannon and musket. The smoke clearing. But this time, the advance continued, the soldiers stepping over their fallen comrades in the first two ranks of the Royalist attack.

'Pikemen, are you ready? First two lines of muskets withdraw, Pikemen step forward.'

'That's us. Come on. Get back.' Sergeant Eyre scrambled from his position followed by the others. A troop of pikemen pushed past to occupy the barricade's front line, silent and grim faced. Incoming fire started to build as the advance got closer. A soldier on the right bank dropped to the floor as he reloaded the cannon. An apprentice boy stood up to replace him and was instantly hit in the chest.

Tom joined a stream of musketeers leaving the bridge, running east towards Old Brentford town, but not in disorderly panic. After twenty yards they stopped, formed a line and started to reload. Ahead of them the bridge now presented a formidable defensive obstacle, bristling with fifteen foot pikes.

Tom was struggling to recharge his musket. He cursed his clumsiness as he struggled to push the musket ball down the barrel.

Sergeant Eyre saw him. 'Don't force it Tom! Try another.' Tom frowned at him, panic rising. 'Half our musket balls are not an even size,' Eyre shouted. 'If it gets stuck inside the top of the barrel, your gun's useless.' Tom cursed his luck. First a misfire and now second-rate ammunition. A good number of other redcoats would be facing similar problems. It was a miracle they were holding firm. He completed the reload, and awaited orders.

Sergeant Eyre put his hands to his mouth and bellowed the command. 'Musketeers. Front line take advance positions on the right bank. Second line, go to the left bank. And prepare to fire, on the captain's command.'

Tom's heart sank. They were re-entering the fray, moving back toward the bridge. He stuck close to Eyre as they ran onto the bank, perfectly positioned to rake the massed flanks of the enemy, now pushing against the barrier. Eyre waved to the captain, who remained on the bridge with the pikemen.

'Wait on me, musketeers.' It was the captain's voice again, in control and command.

‘Second line of pike, disengage, and retreat’.

The mass of King’s troops on the bridge surged forward as half the Parliamentary pikemen ran off the bridge leaving their pikes in position.

‘Musketeers, take aim…and fire!’

A fusillade ripped into both sides of the King’s infantry, causing instant confusion. Many fell and the weight of troopers pressing behind increased the pile up of bodies, living, dead and injured.

‘First line of pike. Disengage and retreat. Musketeers retreat. All forces retreat.’

The remaining redcoats on and around the bridge turned and sprinted down the road to Old Brentford. Tom watched long enough to see how many remained, lying on the ground, before a hand grabbed his shoulder and spun him around.

‘Run Tom. Run for your life!’ and Sergeant Eyre propelled him forward.

The road ahead, curving a little to the right, was full of sprinting troopers, the pikemen, unencumbered by their weapons, taking the lead. He glanced behind him and saw several Royalist soldiers clambering over the barricade. Every step he expected to hear shots ringing out, but at this rate they would soon be beyond effective range.

He ran past a young man helping another to walk. The enemy would engulf them once they’d pushed the barricade aside, and the two were arguing.

‘Leave me be, Benjamin. Save yourself.’

‘I’m going nowhere without you, brother. What would I say to Ma? Now get your arm around me and keep walking.’

The young soldier had been shot in the thigh and his left leg trailed uselessly along the ground. Both would be captured within minutes.

Tom slowed down. He heard Eyre's voice ringing out. 'Nothing you can do for them, Tom. Continue falling back.'

He saw the panic in their faces. Tears were streaming down the cheeks of the older brother as he recognised the hopelessness of their position.

He stopped and confronted the two. 'You have to get off this road. You'll never reach Old Brentford before the King's troops catch up with you.'

'But where do we go, mister? We know every alley around Smithfields but we're lost out here. Are we even near London?'

'There's no time to lose. Here, let me help,' and he supported the injured soldier on his other side and, together, they walked the wounded man off the right side of the road and behind a wooden barn, to the start of a pathway.

'Keep on this path, leaving the road behind you, and head to the Thames. You should come across another track on your right in about quarter of a mile. Take that and you'll see a big manor called Syon House. You'll find help there.'

The troopers looked doubtful. 'Help? At a manor house?' From lords and ladies?'

'It's occupied by Royalist troops. You'll have to dodge the guards on the back way to the kitchens but, once you are there, ask for the cook named Joan. She may be able to give you shelter. Tell her Lady Lucy's friend sent you.' The sound of approaching soldiers was getting louder. 'Now go! Hurry!' and he started sprinting again for Old Brentford. He looked back after fifty yards and saw two small figures in the field behind the barn, slowly heading south, towards the river.

Tom picked up speed and rounded the bend. The road stretched in front in a straight line. More buildings were appearing on both sides and a stream of troopers in scattered bunches were jogging to the relative safety of the second barricade, manned by soldiers in purple coats. Once again it had been well positioned, on a slight crest where houses were close to the road sides. To his right, beyond the buildings, the Thames was visible, rolling past. It would be difficult to outflank this position, which would limit the Royalist options.

Tom reached the barricade and leaned against a wooden barrel breathing in great gulps of air. His lungs ached and his legs were weak. It was good to let go of the musket, which was getting heavier with every step. Sergeant Eyre approached. 'See you avoided capture,' he grumbled. 'It's noble to help your fellow man, but not at the expense of your life. There's a barrel of beer and hot pottage over in that house. Get yourself something to eat and drink and report back here. I'm off to find more ammunition.'

'Who are these men in purple coats?'

'Lord Brooke's regiment of foot, about 400 of them. They're a welcome sight after the numbers we've lost.'

'But where in God's name is the rest of the army? Don't they know we're facing a couple of regiments here, at least?'

'Our commanders were not expecting an attack while King Charles was discussing peace terms. That's why Lord Brooke's not here. You were lucky to catch Denzil Holles. He returned to London before the fighting started. They thought Rupert would only test our defences with a skirmish or two. As far as I know, our artillery has still not been withdrawn.'

'But surely word of this major assault has now reached Parliament?'

'If it has, no doubt they've formed a committee to discuss it,' and Eyre spat into the dust. 'They'll wake up sooner or later but, until then, it's up to us to keep the King at bay, and save our army's cannon.'

Tom went in search of a much-needed drink. His throat was parched. He knew he should eat but had no appetite. Men were milling around the entrance of a house, queuing for hot pottage. A young woman thrust a leather tankard of beer into his hand and Tom drained it in one. He held it out to the woman with a pleading expression. She laughed and filled it again from a jug. Her smile was the first he had seen in days and lifted his spirits. A small, bearded man was standing next to her, inviting more redcoats to join them. 'C'mon men. Fill your bellies. Food with grateful thanks from the people of Brentford, for keeping the looting swine Rupert from our door. We're all behind you.'

Tom gave a wry smile. I'd prefer them in front of us, if we have to face Rupert. Now he smelt the pottage he was famished, and took a bowl from the young woman with thanks. This is something the Royalist army won't be getting, and he surprised himself with a surge of sympathy for the men who would soon be trying to kill him. Days without hot food, shelter or much sleep, constantly on the march towards London and the prospect of death at the hands of the Parliamentary forces. It was enough to dispirit the toughest Royalist soldier.

He returned to Sergeant Eyre who had received their deployment orders. 'Right lads, we're to set up behind the barricade to the left of the road, as it faces west, towards the enemy. Head for the redoubt dug for the cannon. Joseph? How's your face? You recovered?' Joseph nodded quickly, embarrassed he made so much of a light wound.

'Good, we need everyone fit and ready for the next attack. If anyone is completely out of match, ball or powder, see me. I have a little to spare but only come asking if you've nothing left. Tom when you've taken your position, check all your musket balls for any more wrong 'uns. If you find some, tell George. He'll show you what to do.'

They settled behind the barricade and Tom emptied his small pouch of musket balls. Three appeared sufficiently misshapen to cause problems. George sat next to him and took a small pair of iron nippers from his pocket. Without saying a word, he ran his thumb over the ball, trimming small lumps of lead standing proud on the surface. Within minutes he handed them back to Tom with a toothless grin. 'They'll do. Three less of the King's bastards returning to their mothers tonight,' and he scrambled back to his position behind the barricade.

Tom was surprised by George's words. He was not used to the thought of fighting fellow Englishmen, but George clearly had no such qualms. In truth, he probably did it every Saturday night at his local. To George, and many others like him, was this so different?

Sergeant Eyre crouched at his side. 'You're all in, Tom. Close your eyes, say your prayers and you'll be asleep in no time. Grab it while you can. Don't worry, we won't let you miss the entertainment.' Tom gazed at the bustle of organisation, the shout of command and laughter of nervous soldiers. He was certain sleep would evade him but, sensing a moment's relaxation, his exhausted brain took control and, within a minute, closed down his consciousness.

It seemed like only seconds later when he was woken by a gentle shaking of his shoulder. 'Time to stir yourself, Tom. They're on their way.'

His mind struggled to surface from its torpor, his brain protesting with a dull ache behind his eyes. He stiffly scrambled up behind the barricade and peered over the top. A line of soldiers was marching steadily towards them, muskets at the ready. They filled the width of the road, as far as the houses lining each side. Behind them, Tom beheld a sea of bobbing heads and the tops of musket barrels carried in the port arms position. He struggled to take it in. With standard bearers at the front, it was a fearsome but unreal sight. He was shaken out of his daze when, as one, the Royalist troops shouted something he did not understand, then cheered themselves with hoarse, fear-strained voices.

Again, it was infantry only. The possibility of fallen horses blocking the narrow approach would not be risked a second time. Tom looked along the defence line. Lord Brooke's purple coats were concentrated in the middle, flanked on either side by the remains of Denzil Holles's redcoats. They had taken another battering at the bridge and were now a shadow of the force that had proudly presented at Edge Hill. Would they survive this next encounter as a regiment?

A familiar voice rang out. The defence's centre was purple coated but the orders were coming from the redcoat captain. 'Gentlemen. It is my pleasure and honour to command you again, and we welcome Lord Brooke's company to our number.' This was greeted by laughter and cheering. Sprits were high, despite their perilous position. 'Let's give these King's men another taste of their own blood. Stand by to fire, on my order.'

The King's troops were now only thirty yards from the barricade and, following a barked command, they came to a halt. Tom noticed a scuffle as a man broke free from their ranks and wandered towards the barricade, shouting at both sides and waving his pistol.

****

He breathed deeply as he left the King's ranks and approached the Parliamentary barricade. Voices told him to come back, but what for? The game was up. Someone was shouting at him from the defences in front but he did not understand them.

He knew the world was going to the dogs. So he'd gathered his children in, to the safety of his hidden hoard. The little beauties - his emeralds, diamonds, spinels, garnets, cat's eyes, moonstones. The very mention of their names made him certain and strong. Armageddon was coming and when all was over, with the unworthy purged from both sides, he would build a new world around the pure riches he possessed, nature's bounty. But now, all this had been turned to ash. It wasn't meant to end like this, and he tasted bitter tears of frustration running into his gasping mouth.

****

The lone soldier had been spotted by all the defenders and a barrage of cheers and insults reigned down on him. Some were encouraging him to switch sides and join their ranks. Others were shaking their fists or sighting him down their muskets.

Sergeant Eyre shook his head. 'This is the madness we are driven to. The brotherhood of men should follow the Lord and stand firm against commands to fight each other. Look at this poor soul, he's out of his wits.' The man was twenty yards from the barricade, when he stopped and dropped to his knees.

****

Soldiers were everywhere and he was, for a moment, an actor surrounded by his audience. He had come to Brentford in one final, desperate attempt to stop the madness. But he had no words left. The trade he had served for thirty years was corrupted by fakers and tricksters. The venality of man appalled him . The Guild was no better. Once responsible for the upkeep of standards, it was being bled dry by Parliament, always seeking more money. There was nothing left worth fighting for.

He had been driven to employing brutish louts to steal for his precious hoard. But at least, in his case, the means more than justified the ends. He had almost succeeded but always suspected Billy Boy would be his undoing, and so it had proved, for now they would trace him though that fool. Why had he threatened the woman? There had been no need. But the little bully could not resist getting one back on the Tallants.

No matter. Once Billy knows he's been rumbled, he'll either give me up or, more likely, do me in. Either way, I am finished. And, truth be told, I do not deserve any better, running with such vermin.

****

Both sides were now starting to lose patience with the lunatic wandering across their field of fire. Even the Trained Bands, glad of every minute the attack was delayed, were becoming frustrated. They had prepared for battle and were reconciled to their fate. Now they just wanted to get on with it.

'Stand down. Your final warning,' the captain shouted again, remaining calm.

The soldier remained on his knees, talking to himself, then stopped and launched into another stream of shouted insults, cut short by an abrupt shout of command and volley of redcoat musket fire.

****

He was kneeling on the ground, arms outstretched, beseeching both sides to see what they were doing. He noticed puffs of smoke from the muskets in front of him and then a searing pain as a lead ball tore through the palm of his left hand.

A second grazed his midriff. He reached into his jerkin pocket and withdrew the remains of a slim agate cameo, today's amulet, shattered by the shot. Why was it not still whole? What was happening?

A third musket ball ripped into his chest and spun him sideways like a ragdoll, dropping him to the ground in a heap. He lay on his side, gazing at the barricade, the blood from his chest pooling around him. His senses were receding, his vision starting to blur. He squeezed the shards of agate in his right fist as hard as he could, and experienced the welcome pain, keeping his senses alive for a moment longer. He grunted and smiled as the blackness descended. If he couldn't keep his lovelies, no-one else would.

****

Tom looked at the fallen soldier. What torment had driven him to throw his life away?

His thoughts were interrupted by barked commands from the King's lines. 'As you were, men. No more distractions. On my command'. The Royalist infantry facing Tom adjusted their positions in readiness, causing a ripple of movement in their ranks.

'Ready.' The front row kneeled

'Aim.' The kneeling soldiers raised their muskets and sighted the barricade, followed by the second row standing behind them. The combined effect was chilling.

'Down everyone, take shelter…'

'Fire!'

Sergeant Eyre's warning was drowned in a thunderous crash. A hailstorm of splinters hit their faces as the barricade took the full force of the fusillade. Shots whistled overhead like angry hornets and men around Tom fell, but not in great numbers. He heard a roar and peeped from his cover. The King's men were running at them, less than twenty yards away.

'Red and Purple. Take aim…'Fire!'

Tom had no time to aim precisely. He fired into the mass of bodies and dived for cover. 'They're on us!' he shouted at Sergeant Eyre, who nodded and drew his sword.

'Time for pistols, butt ends and cold steel. God be with us!'

The King's men hit the barricade with a crash. A figure appeared wielding a farmer's hook to dislodge a barrel. Eyre slashed him with his sword and the man fell backwards into the melee with a scream, instantly replaced by another.

'Pistol!' Eyre shouted in warning. Joseph rammed the butt end of his musket into the soldier's face but not before he had fired point blank at George who slumped to the floor. 'Damn you,' shouted Eyre and thrust at the soldier as he fell away from the barricade. He stepped over George's body, protecting him.

Tom was aware of movement to their right. 'They've overrun the gun crew in the redoubt and broken through the line! They'll cut us off!

Sergeant Eyre looked over and shouted to Tom. 'I'll hold this position with Andrew. You and Joseph try and push those others back. Tom pulled his pistol and sword from his belt. His fear and anger surged together in a battle rage. Before he knew it, he was charging at the King's men scrambling through the redoubt, screaming at the top of his voice.

A young trooper spun around to face him and was scythed down by Tom's sword. Following up, Joseph cracked the soldier's skull with the end of his musket. A bearded man to their right thrust his sword into Joseph's arm. Tom raised his pistol carefully. He was shooting with his left hand but, at this range, could not miss, and fired into the stomach of the man, who dropped to the floor.

Pausing to return his pistol to his belt, Tom watched the battle unfolding. The Trained Bands were fighting valiantly but sheer force of numbers was forcing them back. Brooke's purple coats were holding firm in the centre but both flanks were starting to buckle. Tom and Joseph had protected Eyre and Andrew from being outflanked but, to his right, the King's troops continued to pour through the breach.

'Sergeant. We will soon be cut off from the rest of the defensive line.'

Eyre wiped a stream of blood from his brow and appraised the situation quickly. 'We've got the enemy massing in front of us and growing numbers on our right, where they've broken though the line. The Thames is on our left, nearing full tide. We'll have to retreat through the buildings behind us, on our left, and join the rearguard of Brookes' men.'

Joseph was back on his feet but his left sleeve was wet with blood. Tom glanced at George's body. Eyre shook his head. 'Leave him. There's nothing we can do.' Sergeant signaled to Andrew and Joseph and they ran to the first building behind them with three other redcoats. 'Some fall back positions have been set up in the lanes which we can defend. Follow me!' Eyre hurtled down the side of the house and entered a narrow road which, twenty yards down' was blockaded by a cart . 'This will do!' and Eyre vaulted the cart and helped a soldier climb over.

'I'm not waiting here,' the boy shouted. He looked no older than sixteen and terrified.

'Stand firm,' Eyre shouted but the trooper slipped through his grasp.

A second soldier jumped over and ran. 'I'm back to London. Stay here and, when the King wins, you'll be dancing from a rope.'

Eyre grabbed the third trooper by the collar. 'You're not joining your friends, are you?' The tall, thin boy looked helpless and shook his head silently. 'That's the spirit. You stay here and we'll defend this position. Everybody primed and ready?'

'I've only got a couple of shots left, sergeant.' Joseph said.

Eyre nodded. 'Make them count.' The noise from the battle continued and Tom could hear men approaching down the alley from the direction of the barricade. Was the defence holding? 'Standby. On my order, fire at will, but only when you're sure you have a clear target, and make sure they're King's men!'

Five soldiers ran around the corner and immediately stopped. The man in front signaled them to crouch while he advanced slowly, looking at the cart carefully. 'We have a small group of roundhead pigs here, lads, who need dealing with.'

Tom recognised the voice and swore loudly. It's Appleyard! Why isn't he at Syon House?

Sergeant Eyre gave him a quizzical look. 'Anything amiss?'

'See the leader of the group? His name's Appleyard. I've only just escaped from him and have no intention of falling into his clutches again.'

'Nasty piece, is he?' Tom nodded. 'Let's make sure he doesn't cause any more trouble.' And without warning Eyre raised his musket, took careful aim and shot at Appleyard, who collapsed to the floor. The other Royalist soldiers flattened themselves on the ground. Appleyard was still and

Tom was about to congratulate Eyre, when he saw the sergeant's foot twitching, and then his leg move.

'Only creased him,' Eyre said, clicking his tongue in frustration. 'Was aiming for his head, so I must have been close.' Appleyard was now shouting for help. Two troopers crawled along the road on their stomachs, grabbed him by his coat and dragged him back along the lane until they rounded the corner and disappeared from view. Eyre looked over his shoulder. 'I can hear voices behind us now. Someone's approaching.'

'If they're Royalist troops, behind our defences, we're trapped,' Tom said.

Eyre nodded. 'We must get off this lane and out of sight. Andrew and Tom, work your way into town, away from the fighting, and try every door on the right side of the alley. Trooper, what's your name?'

The young soldier looked terrified. 'Francis, sir. Francis Middleton.'

'Well Francis, you, Joseph and I will check the left side. Don't worry lad, we'll find a way out. Let's get to work,' and Sergeant Eyre ran across the lane and pushed at the first house door which was firmly locked.

'Come on, Andrew,' Tom shouted. 'A shilling if you find an open door.' The lad's eyes lit up and he set off testing every doorway. The five made rapid progress down the lane, into Old Brentford. Soon the upturned cart was twenty yards behind them. Appleyard had not re-appeared and, despite the earlier voices, there was no sign of anyone approaching from the other direction.

The local people had been expecting trouble and every door was soundly locked. Tom was praying for an opening, to get off the lane, out of sight before they were seen. If they could do that, no-one would know of their existence.

'Wish I could remove this armour,' Andrew exclaimed. 'My body is starting to boil inside.'

Tom saw his face was now crimson and he was short of breath. 'No time, Andrew. Just hang on!'

'Stop there or we shoot!' Tom spun around at the sound he had been dreading, to confront Sergeant Appleyard, the top of his head wrapped in a bloodstained bandage.

'Is that ?… well, I don't believe it! Thomas Tallant, within my grasp again.'

Tom groaned. Appleyard and his men had regrouped, pushed aside the cart and caught up with them. 'Leave the doors. Run for it!', and the five of them put their heads down and, legs pumping, ran along the empty lane into Old Brentford.

Andrew was soon lagging behind. He was exhausted and the realisation that he was falling back increased his panic. His breathing was laboured and several times he tripped and staggered.

'Up ahead, on the right.' It was Francis, the young trooper. 'There's an opening…a track, I think.

'You're right. Reach that and we can make a stand.'

A shot rang out and the whistle of a musket ball passed near Tom's head. Andrew shouted in fear but kept staggering forward, his breath now coming in rasping sobs. There was another shot and Joseph fell in front of Tom, who had to hurdle over his prone body.

Eyre was first to the corner of the lane and track and, as he rounded the bend, he slid to a halt and knelt behind the house's edge, pointing his musket up towards Appleyard's approaching men. He waited until Tom, Francis and eventually Andrew ran past him into the lane.

'Take cover!' he shouted, took a deep breath, steadied his aim and fired. A soldier in front of Appleyard crumpled and fell to the ground. 'Tom, is your musket primed? Let me have it. I will hold them for as long as I can. You get young

Andrew and Francis as far as you can away from here. I'll follow you soon.'

Tom was about to protest but one look at Sergeant Eyre's expression told him to follow orders. 'Here, have my pistol too.'

'No, you'll need it. I have my own. Now go. You're losing precious seconds.'

Tom swapped his musket for Eyre's and pushed the two lads stumbling down a rough path towards a field. He glanced over his shoulder to see Eyre pressed against the wall, settling into a shooting position.

The track was lined with walls on both sides but soon led to flat open country. The noise of battle receded as they ran and the peaceful scene ahead brought Tom up short. A shaft of thin sunlight broke though the grey cloud and he saw movement ahead, on the near horizon.

It was the river. They were approaching the northern bank of the Thames, its great mass of water sliding downstream towards London, with the tide on the turn. They continued through the fields to the river's edge. To his right, Tom saw the distinctive shape of Syon House. To his left the churning water curved right, passing Kew on the south bank before disappearing from view on its journey past Mortlake and Chiswick.

Tom considered the options. Ahead, the Thames. To their right, Syon House. Heading left would take them back towards Old Brentford. If they went that way, but remained on the outskirts, they might edge past the fighting and rejoin Brooke's men waiting in reserve. It seemed the only possible route.

Andrew had recovered his breath and was tugging at the straps holding his breastplate in place. 'Can't wear this no longer,' he grunted as he pulled at the armour.

'Think on how it's saved your life,' said Tom, pointing at the mark made by the musket ball. 'We're not out of danger yet.' Andrew stopped and sat quietly, a sulky expression on his usually cheerful face. Tom pictured him back at the warehouse, tending Meg in the stable. Such normality was a world away and he missed it terribly. Tom saw they had stumbled on a sanctuary of calm amongst the chaos. The sound of battle had receded and he could hear birdsong. It was tempting to sit there and let the world flow by, like the Thames.

Then he heard a familiar sound. A low drumming – horses at full gallop. A group of riders was heading towards them from Syon House. 'Down everyone!'

Francis appeared from a behind a shrub pulling up his breeches. 'Francis,' Tom called louder. 'Riders approaching. Get down!'

It was too late. One of the horsemen spotted the young trooper's redcoat and pulled to a halt, pointing and shouting. Within seconds they were off again, building speed, but now riding directly at them. 'Sweet Jesu. Now we're in trouble.' Tom cursed. 'Run, both of you. As fast as you can!' If they were caught by a troop of cavalry on open ground, their end was assured. Their only hope was to find an obstacle to stop the horses to even the odds, if only by a little.

'The river. Head for the river!'

They ran along the track towards the river bank, tall grasses pulling at their legs. A startled grey heron flew upwards from under their feet. Andrew was starting to fall back again. Tom saw he was near the end of his tether. The riders were eating up the ground between them. Tom was now able to see the river more clearly, and something he hadn't expected.

It was a small island. In fact there were three, long and thin, each in succession shadowing the north bank of the Thames. The channel of water between the first island and the riverbank was narrow. Might they cross it? He pointed to the island and the water running swiftly in front of him. How deep was it?

He heard a shout behind him. The riders were slowing as they approached. 'Stand still, there. Don't move.' The men came to a halt ten yards away. 'Redcoats, eh? Thought we'd finished you off at Edge Hill.' Tom stood at the river bank, judging the river's speed and depth. 'Come lads. You won't attempt to cross to that island, surely? You fought bravely at Kineton. Don't throw your life away now. The river is in flood.'

Tom studied the cavalry officer who was talking. He sounded reasonable but he didn't trust the others, leaning forward in their saddles and grinning at each other. If we surrendered, how would we be treated? Francis whispered in his ear. 'I know this place. My uncle was a basket weaver and said this island grows the best willow. I used to help him carry it home. When the river is low there's one place you can walk across.'

'Can you remember where it is?'

'I believe so.'

Francis stared at Tom, saying nothing. He's waiting for me to tell him what to do, Tom thought. He studied the river sliding past. He doubted the cavalry men would risk their horses on such a crossing. It was their only chance to escape.

The riders were losing their patience. 'Let's finish them off and be done with it,' one called to the officer. 'Three fewer roundheads will make England a better place.'

Tom raised Eyre's empty musket and sighted the man down his barrel. 'One step forward and I will take you with me. Francis, leave your musket and knapsack here and test the water. If you're getting out of your depth, come back.' He watched the lad do what he was told. He's placing his life totally in my hands, Tom thought. I should go first but

Andrew and Francis would not last a minute against these Royalists.

'What do you think, James? I'll wager a crown he'll be swept away.'

James lent on the pommel of his saddle, an unpleasant smile on his face. 'I like the look of my man. He's tall and has form. Knows the course. You're on.'

Tom was glad of the distraction but felt disgust for these men.

All watched as Francis carefully waded into the river opposite the western tip of the island where the distance was less. He'd taken off his shoes, to help his feet grip the river floor. He was soon up to his knees and the flowing water was buffeting his legs. He's not a quarter across yet. This isn't going to work.

Francis pressed on, the swell of water rising rapidly up his body. He suddenly fell forward, losing his balance, his shoulder dipping under the surface. If he misses his footing he'll be gone, Tom thought, but the young trooper steadied himself, regaining his balance and courage.

'Come, this is getting tedious. Get on with it.'

'It's not a race, Louis. Leave him be. Come on young fellow. I have a crown on you. Keep going!'

Francis had his back to them, ignoring the urgings of the soldiers. With every step he was growing in Tom's estimation. And then, in seconds, it was over. Francis had found rising ground underfoot. His body, dripping with water started to emerge from the river and two steps later he pulled himself onto the island's bank. James and his friends cheered while others started to complain. For precious moments, Tom and Andrew had been forgotten and he pulled his groom towards him. He was shaking.

'I can't do it, Master. I can't swim!'

'I doubt Francis can, but he had no choice, and neither do we. Think of the tales we'll be able to tell Isaac. How we escaped the King's cavalry!'

At the mention of Isaac's name a thin smile crossed the lad's face and he nodded. 'That's it. Come on. I'll be right behind you,' and he pulled him by the arm to the river bank. In seconds they were in the river, following the route taken by Francis. They were now at the soldiers' mercy but Tom hoped the horsemen's gambling instinct would save them. And so it proved.

'Oh, look Louis, they're off again. I'll wager my winnings these two will make it as well.'

'One of them is shorter than the first redcoat. I'll take your bet.'

Within seconds of entering the river, Tom knew they were in trouble. Andrew could hardly move, stricken with fear and the water was colder than Tom expected. He grabbed the young man's arms from behind and encouraged him gently forward. The current was relentless, pushing past them and soon Tom was losing sensation in his legs.

'We have to keep moving, and more quickly. Think of Sam and Mistress Elizabeth. They'll be so proud of you!' The mention of Elizabeth's name stirred the young lad back into life and he took a determined step forward.

In a second, he was gone. He had missed his footing and disappeared into the swirling water. There was a cheer from the bank and Tom cursed the soldiers. In one movement, he steadied himself and launched his arms forward under the churning surface. He found something…an arm, and Tom pulled with all his strength while bracing his body against the continuous battering of the current.

He hauled Andrew's arm towards him and saw something fair-coloured beneath the surface. His hair. He grabbed at it with his other hand and Andrew's face broke the surface, coughing and spluttering. They were less than half way across the river and from the corner of his eye he saw Francis clinging onto a tuft of grass on the bank, his arm extended in a hopeless gesture of help.

Andrew was lying on the surface, Tom hanging onto his arm, lifting his mouth clear of the water. His legs were pushing against the current, carrying the weight of both himself and Andrew. He could no longer feel his feet. He tried to pull Andrew closer, to hold him around his chest. But why was it such a struggle? The extreme cold was sapping his strength, but it was more than that. With an enormous effort he pulled Andrew closer. His arm hit something hard and his heart sank. Andrew was wearing his breastplate under his coat and its weight was pulling him down.

Desperately Tom tried to unstrap its buckles but the effort made him teeter over and his right foot slipped on the river bank. Immediately, they were both pushed further along the channel between the bank and island, as Tom desperately tried to keep hold of his young friend while finding fresh purchase with his frozen feet. His left foot touched a solid surface and he instinctively pushed it down into the mud, scraping his ankle raw on the side of a stone. His waist and chest muscles were burning as he strained to keep the lad upright against the relentless force of the river.

He looked at Andrew's upturned face, close to his. His eyes were open but he said nothing. 'I need you to help me untie your breastplate. I can't do it on my own.' Andrew lifted his right arm feebly and pawed at his coat, but then shook his head and stopped. Still the river pounded past them, and the men's cheers continued.

Tom's mind recalled another time, in the river Thames, gripping a rope to stay alive but knowing he wouldn't hold on much longer. The river was pulling Andrew away. If it would only stop, for one minute, he was close enough to the bank to carry his friend there, he was sure of it. But it wouldn't, and he couldn't.

He cursed himself. Why did he tell him to keep his armour, when he complained about the heat? A sudden eddy of water loosened Tom's grip and Andrew was pushed away from him. He grabbed at his arm and hung on. His eyes were open and, if he could still see, he would know his master was crying with frustration, exhaustion and the pain of imminent loss. The moment came. He had to let go, completely spent, and watched in despair as Andrew Lamkin's face, staring at him, sped away, disappearing from view for ever.

Tom was finished. He stood still, in a daze, and tried to breathe. He knew he must reach dry land but wasn't able to move. The island was too far away, now he'd lost his strength. A rousing cheer from the bank brutally brought him to his senses and hot anger revitalized his body. He *would* get back to the river bank if only to confront those bastards who were making sport of Andrew's death. Carefully, Tom turned and moved towards the cavalry men, eventually striding clear of the water, feeling his strength come back. Reaching the bank, he was met by James towering above him, mounted on his horse.

'You have lost me a crown,' he snarled, 'more than enough to cost you your life,' and he drew a pistol from its saddle holster.

'Come James, leave him be. You've had your sport and we need to move on.'

'Not until I have dealt with this roundhead dog,' and he cocked the pistol and raised it to take aim.

'We've been ordered to scout the Parliamentary positions and report back. It will soon be dark. We have no time for this.'

'It will only take a moment…all that remains of your life, roundhead. A moment.'

Tom closed his eyes and thought of Elizabeth.

A shot rang out.

'Damnation!'

Tom opened his eyes to see the cavalier had wheeled his horse and was looking away from the river, towards the barricaded road. He saw a puff of smoke and, a second later, heard another shot. One of the horses reared up, dismounting its rider, who shouted 'my horse has been hit!'. Redcoats in the distance were running towards them, among them the unmistakable figure of Sergeant Eyre. With the cavalrymen distracted, Tom pulled himself on to the bank, scrambled over to his pistol and aimed at James.

'You should go, as your friend suggested. You are no longer master of this situation'. He cocked the pistol and held it steady, pointing at the horseman's head.

'We have to leave. My horse is bleeding badly. It will not carry me much further!'

The cavalrymen watched the approaching redcoats and, after a second's hesitation, set off back to the Royalist lines. As he left, James looked over his shoulder with a grim smile. 'You have the luck of the devil, roundhead. Until next time!' and, slapping his horse's shoulder, galloped after the others.

Tom's legs buckled beneath him and he sat on the grass. The pistol was shaking in his hand, his breath coming in tight bursts. Francis was jumping up and down on the island, waving at the approaching redcoats. Tom looked past Francis at something out in the middle of the river. It was another figure, also waving but this time in panicked despair, as it was swept away by the strong current. Then he saw another, face down in the water, and more still coming from his right, their recoats bobbing on the surface like fallen cherries. The defences at Old Brentford must have finally been overrun. The only escape for some was the river, but that was no escape at all.

His head filled with the vision of Andrew's face, eyes open, disappearing with them down the Thames, and he lowered his head and sobbed.

Chapter 33

Turnham Green

Tom stared into the flames, lost to the world. A green jacketed soldier gently shook his arm and handed over a bowl of pottage. Tom took the food and nodded. He was too exhausted to eat, but maybe later.

Sergeant Eyre walked over and sat beside him. 'Been checking this fire's nowhere near the ammunition wagons,' Eyre grunted. 'You'd think gunners would know that but I've seen more stupid mistakes made. But the warmth is welcome.' He extended his palms out to the fire as Tom looked up into the stars. To his left a dull glow lit the night sky. Old Brentford was burning.

'Rupert's men are enjoying themselves,' he said absently to Eyre, keeping his eyes on the glow.

'Yes. The bastards will be running amok, stealing what they can from the townsfolk and burning the rest. Poor sods. They had us ransacking their houses for ammunition this morning and now it's the King's men turning them over!'

'It's Rupert's warning to London, isn't it? This is the price of opposing my uncle, your King, standing in the way of his progress back to the capital.'

'Well, if he's got any sense he'll curb his nephew's enthusiasm. If the Trained Bands think this is what London faces, it will stiffen their resolve.'

Tom looked at the corralled guns and wagons of the artillery train surrounding them. 'Where's the army?'

'If you can believe it, they still haven't sent reinforcements. I don't understand it.'

Tom shook his head. 'What happened after we were separated in the lane?'

'I held my covering position on the corner, as you set off for the river. Your friend Appleyard was slowly advancing from behind that cart on my left when soldiers appeared in the lane from my right. I thought I was surrounded, but it was half a dozen battered redcoats, inching their way towards me like lost sheep.

Greencoats from John Hampden's regiment of foot had moved up to defend the barricade. They told the boys to retreat out of the town while they held the line, but this group took a wrong turn and got lost in the side streets, thank God. They were scared shitless, expecting to run into the Royalist army at any moment. They were certainly glad to see me.

'So what did you do?'

'I got them organised to defend the corner. We had a bit of a stand-off with Appleyard but pushed up on his men and a couple of smart volleys from my boys saw them off. Then we came searching for you. I'm sorry you lost Andrew, he was a good lad.'

Tom nodded, staring into the fire. 'As you know, we formed a chain across the channel to rescue Francis from the island,' Tom continued. The young soldier looked up from the other side of the fire and grinned. 'God only knows how you crossed on your own, Francis. Stronger than you look, aren't you?

'He had more luck than the other poor souls who perished in the Thames,' Eyre grimaced. 'Those brave boys put up such a fight, only to be drowned like rats. I pray for their souls.'

'And our luck held, as we cut across country and reached Turnham Green without meeting any more cavalry. We had a very close escape.'

'It is God's will, as is the survival of the guns, still so poorly defended.'

'Yes, if night hadn't descended, and Rupert had ignored the booty in Brentford, my Lord Essex's artillery would now be in the King's hands. So, when the morning comes, what forces do we have left to face the King?'

'The greens and the purples of Hampden and Brookes and what's left of our redcoats, but we are now pitifully few.'

'Against the entire King's army? Where in God's name is Essex?'

Eyre stood up and stretched. 'I will pray to the Lord for a satisfactory answer to your question. But now me must get what sleep we can, and prepare ourselves for tomorrow, and what may be our final day on God's good earth, and the glory to follow.'

Although exhausted, sleep eluded Tom. The ground was cold and hard and the prospect of what awaited them in the morning pre-occupied him. At least they now had enough ammunition, so he wouldn't die without a fight. He thought of Elizabeth and his family, how their lives would continue without him and his heart ached.

By first light, the fog had returned. Sergeant Eyre was busy, foraging for breakfast. He came back with a mug of ale and corner of bread. Sitting by the fire's ashes, Tom swallowed the ale gratefully but had no stomach for the bread.

'Get it down you. You'll need more than ale in your belly today.' It was a dawn of fear for them all and Eyre's voice was quiet and gentle. The sergeant raised the others. 'Up you get boys. Time to give the King's men another beating. Stock up with powder, match and shot. We can't greet those

Royalists empty handed now, can we?' This was greeted with a murmur of laughter as the men rose, stretched and prepared for the day, glad to have jobs to occupy their mind.

Eyre turned to Tom. 'I've spoken to the captain. Our regiment is in tatters. So what's left of us will stand with Brooke's men on either flank of Hampden's green coats who will occupy the centre ground. I'm expecting some pieces of artillery will be prepared and drawn forward to strengthen our position. They should be here by now. Where have they gone?'

As the sky lightened, Tom got his first sighting of their position. It was hopeless. They no longer had the hedges and narrow lanes around Brentford, which had limited the King's attacking front. As he stared west, from where the Royalist army would come, he saw the village of Turnham Green to his right, but the ground to his left was open and beyond the fog lay Chiswick Common, leading down to the Thames. It was impossible to defend with their tiny force, especially as Prince Rupert would finally be able to bring his full cavalry to bear.

Tom turned to the sergeant who studied his stony expression. 'I know, Tom. We're fucked. We must hold our position here at Turnham Green as long as possible and pray somebody in London has finally woken up and raised the alarm.' Tom thought about the Lines of Communication, the string of defences hastily erected around the city by the people of London. He would give anything to be standing behind them now.

He did not feel scared, only sad and weary. Through an opening in the mist above him, a lone red kite soared into view, its forked tail visible against the white cloud. It kept still, suspended in the sky, watching him. Elizabeth was close, but that brought him anguish, not strength. He had thought of them always being together, but now they would be cut apart forever by a cavalry sword.

'Line up!' The call from Sergeant Eyre crashed through his thoughts. He resented it. Why should he die now, when he had never had more to live for. The rest of Eyre's words were lost to him and he dumbly followed the other men to their position in the defensive line.

There was no cover. He reached a patchy hedge south of the village and was ordered to crouch behind it. It made yesterday's barricade look like a fortress.

He no longer cared. Let's get this over with. Ahead of him, the mist eddied. A breeze was getting up and soon it would be blown away.

He could hear the jingle of horse's bridles coming through the fog and the bark of orders. The Royalists were moving up for the final assault. Of course they were. They knew the few hundred infantrymen before them would be overrun in minutes, and were eager for battle. Stone cold certainty settled in his heart and he was surprisingly calm.

The men were silent, lost in their own thoughts. It was not the time for shouts of encouragement or jokes to keep their spirits up. All knew what awaited them when the curtain of fog parted. After twenty minutes of unseen activity, silence descended and then, on a single command, the King's army stepped forward, out of the dispersing mist.

Tom caught his breath. Three hundred yards away, the ground was filling with a mass of Royalist soldiers. They were forming up in their thousands, infantry and cavalry stretching from the hedge line north of Turnham Green, down across Chiswick Common to the northern banks of the Thames.

On another command, they came to a halt, and waited silently confronting the small patchwork of green, purple and red coated soldiers, gathered in a semicircle at the entrance to Turnham village. The cavalry horses tossed their heads impatiently, eager to start. In an instant, all hope within the defenders was crushed, snuffed out by the brutal reality of what they now faced.

'Perhaps they will spare us? Maybe march around us and on to London?'

It was Francis, who had rarely left Tom's side since yesterday's escape onto the island.

'I think we killed too many of their comrades yesterday for that to happen, Francis. They'll advance all right, but it will only be to surround us and obtain our surrender.' If only, Tom thought, but I must shield the boy from his fate.

Another ten minutes passed. The lack of movement by the King's army made Tom angry. 'Why don't they just get it over with. They're playing with us, like a cat with a mouse, the bastards.' He suddenly remembered the charge by one lone Royalist soldier at the bridge yesterday. He had been surprised by such a futile gesture, but now understood the strain of waiting in a battle line, and what it could do.

He noticed several officers had ridden forward from the King's ranks, pointing and talking. Soon they were joined by another horseman who galloped the length of the army's front, assembled on Chiswick Common.

Sergeant Eyre, crouching next to him behind the hedge, gave him a mystified shrug. The men were talking now. One or two stood up for a better view.

'Hold your positions!' Eyre shouted. 'Nobody move unless I tell you. Keep your heads down.'

The mist was now clearing, revealing a sea of Royalist soldiers. It was impossible to estimate how many. Ten thousand? What the hell were they waiting for?

A new sound was carried on the growing breeze. What was it? Not loud or strong but it raised a foreign sensation in his heart…what was it, expectancy? No, it was hope. It was bloody well hope. He could hear cheering.

He darted a glance at Eyre. 'Who's that?'

But Eyre had his back to Tom. Despite his orders to his troops, Eyre was standing up staring at the lane coming from London.

'Sweet Jesu. I don't believe it.'

A familiar figure was approaching on horseback, through the rear ranks of their defensive line.

'Good morrow, Sergeant Eyre…and Mr.Tallant. I'm glad you've made each other's acquaintance.'

Philip Skippon, followed by a small group of officers, stopped and dismounted. He approached, removed his glove and shook both of them by the hand. 'I expect you have seen hot action and I thank you for your resolute defence. You have saved the Parliamentary artillery from capture, there can be little doubt of that.'

'But why…how are you here, Sir? You're in great danger! We are surrounded.' Eyre stammered.

'I doubt it sergeant. I have brought a few others with me. Six regiments of our trained bands and most of my Lord Essex's army as well, for good measure.' He surveyed the mass of Royalist soldiers before them. 'Yes, the enemy is numerous, but as nothing to our force which I would put at over twenty thousand. The King is a cautious man. I am certain he will weigh up the odds, look at his battle weary soldiers, short of powder, shot and food, and retire from the field to fight another day.

Behind him, across Chiswick Common, a vast line of Parliamentary soldiers was moving forwards to positions on their left. To his right, the banks to the north of Turnham village were filling with thousands more troops. London had finally delivered. The army had been mustered…and what an army!

'We thought you were never coming…' Tom whispered.

'Beggin' you pardon, Sir. What Mr.Tallant means is we did not know when the troops would arrive, but we were ready to repel the King and his men again.'

Skippon smiled and grasped Eyre's shoulder. 'I think if I had been in your position I might have started to doubt. We were caught out by the King's offer to parley. Your regiments were intended to guard only against skirmishers or spying missions. Even your commanders Mr. Holles and Lord Brooke had returned to Parliament to discuss our next move.

'But when word arrived that the King's army was at the doors of Brentford, intent on attack…well, I have never seen the like. The Trained Bands mustered but we weren't able to reach the western road out of London because of the press of people, ordinary citizens, rushing to the newly built defences, armed with whatever they were able to find. If I ever doubted the people's appetite for challenging the King, I no longer can.

'You'll see for yourself when you leave the front line, as you must do now. Your work is done, for the moment. You have earned your rest, and you need some sustenance by the look of you. You'll find many at the gates of London ready to provide it. Gentlemen, prepare for a hero's welcome!'

But Mr. Skippon, I also have news of the gunpowder smuggling…'

'John Pym has briefed me on the success of your mission, Tallant. News of the explosion soon spread and Lady Carlisle was informed about the source of the gunpowder by one of her Royal connections, as she put it. The mill on Hounslow Heath has been raided and the royal sympathisers arrested.'

Tom could see Barty's hand in this. Returning from Colnbrook with Tom's news about the mill, as a supporter of the King his old friend would be reluctant to inform Skippon or Pym. Better to give this juicy morsel to Lucy, who would snap it up, and waste no time increasing her standing with the Puritan leader by sharing it with him. This, in turn, would put Lucy in Barty's debt, never a bad thing. The cunning old fox.

'So, I congratulate you on a complete success,' Skippon continued, 'and can only apologise that my contribution only hindered your investigation.'

'Henry Appleyard?'

'Yes, the traitor. I'm afraid we've had a number of such cases, royal agents infiltrating our ranks, but I would have put money on Appleyard's loyalty. It has been a harsh lesson for me. Was he killed in the fighting?'

Tom shook his head. 'It's difficult to know sir. Not at our hands at least.'

'Well, we will keep our eyes open for Mr. Appleyard in the future. I must now report to my Lord Essex on next steps. Well done again, Tallant. I'm obliged to you, sir.'

Skippon turned to remount and gave them a salute before galloping towards the growing masses of Parliamentary troops moving on to the Common.

Tom stepped towards Eyre and they hugged each other. His mind replayed scenes from the last day…cowering behind the church pew as it was hammered by musket fire, the desperate hand-to-hand fighting as their lines were breached, sprinting down the main street away from the King's army, nearly drowning in the Thames as he tried to help poor Andrew.

It was impossible they had survived. But they had, as had his future life with Elizabeth. Tom thought his heart would burst with happiness.

'I see you made it, Tallant. You're made of stronger stuff than I thought.'

It was Culpeper, striding forward from a troop of advancing soldiers. For the only time in his life, Tom was delighted to see him, because by his side he saw Elizabeth running towards him.

They embraced, as tight as they possible, their faces wet with tears. No words were spoken. They just needed to be sure that it was true. They were together again. Alive and well.

They left the others to walk past the houses and down an alley Tom knew would take them towards the river. Away from the crowds, they sat on a stretch of meadow and just looked at each other in wonder.

'I have missed you so much,' Tom whispered.

'I think we have both been busy,' Elizabeth replied, reaching over and stroking Tom's hair. 'We have much to share.'

'Did you reach Edge Hill? Did you witness the battle?'

Elizabeth nodded but said nothing. Once again tears formed in her eyes. 'Later, I will tell you what I can, when I am ready. It has had a profound effect on me, Tom. Not necessarily for the better.'

Tom frowned but said nothing.

'But, for now, I need to know something,' she continued, 'and it will seem like a strange question. Tom, did you observe anyone during the battle at Brentford who appeared to have no regard for his life. Who acted…as if they wanted to die?'

Tom thought instantly of the King's soldier who advanced alone towards the barricades, ignoring all commands to stop. 'Well I've witnessed much these past weeks but one man in particular stands out. It was yesterday. At one point, I though he was willing us to kill him. He broke from the King's ranks in advance of a line of attack, and tried to take us on all on his own, waving a pistol at us. Come to think of it, I don't think he fired it in the end.'

'And did he…did he walk with a limp, his left leg.'

'Yes, he did. It all added to his rather odd demeanor. I felt sorry for him, actually. Elizabeth, why are you asking he this?'

She looked up at the sky and uttered a large sigh. 'It is as I thought. His name is Robert Cooke and I'm beginning to believe I drove him to his death.'

'What are you saying? What do you mean?'

'It is a long story which I will share with you later. But yesterday, without realising it, I as good as told him I could soon prove he was a jewel thief working with a brutal London gang.'

'Robert Cooke, from the Goldsmith's Guild? A jewel thief?'

'Yes, and when I tell you his accomplice is Billy Boy, you'll see how far he had fallen.'

Tom whistled. 'Billy Boy. There's someone I'd like to catch up with. But what do you mean, you didn't realise you'd told him?'

'It's hard to explain. I was…not myself at the time. As I say, I have a lot to share with you. You just need to give me some time.'

Tom squeezed her hand. 'Yes, time together. That's what I'm going to treasure.'

Elizabeth smiled. 'But don't think too badly of Robert', she added, and pulled a small black satin pouch from her pocket. 'Put your hand out.' And as she opened the pouch, a flash of the purest blue landed on Tom's palm.

'What a sapphire!' he exclaimed. 'Such colour, and it looks flawless.'

'I am sure it is, but unfortunately it's going to Lucy Carlisle.'

'Why? She's got too many gemstones already!'

'Again, that's for another time. The jewel was delivered this morning. No message but it told me Robert was the thief. However, by gifting me this sapphire, he's rescued me from a world of trouble.

'And he's telling me something else. He's saying there's more where this came from.'

Elizabeth held the sapphire to the light between her finger and thumb. The gemstone was alive, winking and sparkling in the morning sun.

'But the question is, Robert, where have you hidden it?'

Chapter 34

London, 371 years later
October 2013
Taken from The Guardian newspaper

Cheapside Hoard of Treasure found in London a century ago, goes on show at the London Museum

For the first time since it was found more than a century ago, the entire glittering Cheapside Hoard has gone on display at the Museum of London.

The largest hoard of Tudor and Jacobean jewellery ever found – almost 500 pieces of extraordinary rarity and beauty – was unearthed in 1912 by the pickaxes of London workmen demolishing an old jeweller's premises in Cheapside in the City of London, a stroll from the present site of the museum.

They stuffed the loot – emeralds, diamonds, rubies and sapphires – some dating back 1,500 years to Byzantium, into pockets, hats and knotted handkerchiefs and took it to "Stony Jack", George Fabian Lawrence, an enigmatic character who ran a pawn shop and acquired objects for museums. He was known to pay workmen cash down, no questions asked, for any interesting finds.

After a dust-up between several London museums about who should get the treasure, most of it went to the new London Museum, and there was a sensation when it opened in 1914 displaying some of the pieces, including a watch set into a single emerald the size of a small apple.

When the first world war broke out, the treasure went into storage, and the whole collection never again came out of its bank vault, until the new exhibition – where visitors enter through a barred gateway, and which is watched over by 24-hour security. Many of the pieces, including pendants, earrings, and the exquisite chains, are displayed suspended in the cases, glittering in lighting intended to emulate the candlelight in which many of them would have been worn.

The remaining mystery is who buried the treasure, and why it was never recovered – although the Great Fire of London, which reduced the shops of Goldsmith's Row to ashes but left the treasure untouched in the cellar, may be the explanation.

Historical Note

As with Thomas Tallant's two previous adventures, 'The Drums of War' is built around a series of actual events during the outbreak of the English Civil War in 1642.

The Battle of Edgehill (or Edge Hill or Kineton Fight, as it was variously called at the time) is well known in Civil War history, less so the fighting in and around Brentford, which arguably was strategically more important. Brentford was the King's last, and best, opportunity to retake London, although he did not realise it at the time.

As usual, Tom and Elizabeth rub shoulders with a sprinkling of real historical figures in pursuit of their adventures. Readers of 'The Wrecking Storm' will know that Lucy Carlisle did exist and now we learn of her links to Syon House, also true. Philip Skippon was the well respected commander of the Trained Bands and Sergeant Eyres is loosely based on a figure from the Levellers Movement who fought at Brentford. However, in every case, their involvement in escapades, from jewel thefts to foiling assassinations, are creations of my imagination (although, perhaps surprisingly, Harvey did look after the King's children during the battle at Edgehill).

Most importantly, I can vouch that the stars of the show – the exquisite collection of Tudor and Stuart jewels – are very real. I have had the pleasure of seeing them with my own eyes. If you ever get this opportunity in the future, take it. It is an unforgettable experience. What if you were gazing upon the jewels so carefully hidden by Robert Cooke?

Looking at the Civil War now, it's easy to make assumptions about people's knowledge of events at the time. In fact contemporary accounts reveal confusion and disbelief about what was happening and why, followed by an acute sense of shock on both sides when they finally unleashed the human destruction of Edgehill - a sense of 'what have we done?'

For more about the history, I would recommend:

London's Lost Jewel's, The Cheapside Hoard by Hazel Forsyth

Circulation – William Harvey's Revolutionary Idea by Thomas Wright

For more about the Tallant family, including details of their first adventure 'Rags of Time', visit www.thomastallant.com .

I always like to hear from the readers of my books. You can contact me via michaelward@thomastallant.com .

Michael Ward

Printed in Great Britain
by Amazon

12957903R00137